PINTO LOWERY

AN EVANS NOVEL OF THE WEST

PINTO LOWERY

G. CLIFTON WISLER

M. EVANS & COMPANY, INC. NEW YORK

Library of Congress Cataloging-in-Publication Data

Wisler, G. Clifton
Pinto Lowery / by G. Clifton Wisler.
p. cm.—(An Evans novel of the West)
ISBN 0-87131-634-x : $15.95
I. Title. II. Series.
PS3573.I877P56 1991 90-25766
813'.54—dc20 CIP

M. Evans and Company, Inc.
216 East 49th Street
New York, New York 10017

Manufactured in the United States of America

9 8 7 6 5 4 3 2 1

All that I am, all that I know,
flows from those who have molded me.

For Elnora Higgins,
my grandmother

Chapter 1

You couldn't call Hill's Junction a town. No, that would've been a stretch. It was just a meeting of roads where a few folks had chosen to build their houses. A fellow named Robertson had set up a store there a year or so after the first settlers came, and Elroy Tubbs had started up his livery and freight business after that. In all, there were close to a dozen buildings now—weathered post oak pickets and pine planks mostly, with nary a splash of paint on the whole lot. In the gray mists of the February morning, Hill's Junction seemed to rise like a phantom from the Texas plain.

Pinto Lowery eyed the swirling fog with suspicion. Back in Marshall, growing up, his ancient grandmother would have tossed chicken bones on a table and read the omens. In Lowery's experience, anytime you couldn't see what rested down the road was a time to stand up and take notice. Plenty of times, fighting with Hood in Virginia, the Yanks had come out of a mist, flags waving, and lashed into the Marshall Guards like a pack of winter-starved range dogs.

That war's over now, he thought as he satisfied himself that the hire horses in the corral had enough oats in their feed trough.

He was turning back toward the barn when a door groaned on its hinges, and a shaggy yellow-haired boy of fourteen stepped outside.

"Feels odd, don't it, Pinto?" the boy asked.

"Jus' frog spit's all," Pinto said, grinning. "Sign winter's passin', Muley."

"I won't cry over that. No, sir," Muley Bryant said, scratching the bare quarter of shoulder left exposed by a pair of overalls a size and a half too large and blowing a tune through an old tin mouth-organ.

"Catch a fever takin' de mornin' air witout a shirt," Pinto scolded. "Miz Dubbs scrubbed that flannel one las' week. Ain't oudgrowed it, have you?"

"No, but it's tight just the same. Chafes the fool out o' my arms. And other places besides."

"Maybe I'll shoot up a deer and make you a Comanche breech-clout," Pinto offered. "Dat or we could jus' leave you oud for dem bucks do snatch some night."

"Wouldn't be much worse'n slavin' for Elroy Tubbs," Muley grumbled. "Only thing keeps me here's your promise I can chase mustangs with you come summer."

"I never promised dat."

"Maybe no, but you'll let me come along just the same. I'm good company."

"Good fer aggravation," Pinto muttered, shooing the youngster back inside. "Now let's ged along after dis work. Got wagons due in today, and we'll be all afternoon unloadin'."

"And all the mornin' workin' these fool horses," Muley said, wiping his brow. "If Miz Tubbs wasn't such a fine cook, I'd . . ."

"You'd have to find yerself a new pair o' britches," Pinto said, laughing as he pulled at one of the oversized legs. "Or else get yerself a twin to share dem pants."

"We can't all o' us match you for style," Muley replied, pointing to the odd assortment of patches that held Pinto's wool trousers and homespun cotton shirt together. His boots were new, cut from fresh cowhide by his own hands and sewn with proper needle and lace. Why not? Before turning to chasing range ponies, George Preston Lowery had labored a whole year stitching boots and saddles at a Victoria factory.

"Guess dey ain't much to look at," Pinto admitted. "But den I don't spend my mornin's at de Governor's Ball."

Muley laughed at the notion, then began scooping oats into feed bags. Elroy Tubbs kept the draft horses in stalls, and they wanted feeding just like the ones outside. As for Pinto, he had himself a look after a roan gelding with a bad front foot. He was still working on the horse when Tom and Ted Tubbs climbed up and sat on the wall of the animal's stall.

"Mornin', Pinto," twelve-year-old Tom called as he yawned. "Looks like a storm's comin'."

Ten-year-old Ted nodded shyly.

"Be a storm sure enough if your ma finds you climbin' stalls in yer school clothes. Thought you'd be on yer way to Miz Pritchard's by now."

"She's sendin' a wagon today," Tom explained. "Now the Franklin boys and Sarah Mills's comin' along. Makes six, what with Alice."

"I figured Alice to have all the educatin' anybody could abide," Muley called from the far side of the barn. "Girl's powerful smart already. Puts me to shame."

"That ain't sayin' so much," Tom remarked. "You could take some lessons, too, Muley."

"Nobody's goin' to educate me!" the stableboy objected. "I'm chasin' mustangs soon as Pinto says the weather's changed."

"Wish I could," Ted said, moaning. "Don't guess you'd take me, would you, Pinto?"

"I did, I wouldn't have just Comanches after my hair. Yer ma'd scalp me sure."

The Tubbs boys laughed at the notion. Pinto just went on working.

"Got a tale for us today?" Tom asked after a time. "Bout the war, maybe? Seen that scar on your hand plenty o' times, but you never tell us how you got it."

"Was at Sharpsburg as I heard it," Muley answered. "But he's mum about it. Get him to talk 'bout horses. He don't altogether mind that."

"Pinto?" Tom asked hopefully.

"Well, dere is one story I recall," Pinto said as he worked the stiffness out of the roan's tendons. "I was thirteen, jus' a hair older'n Tom here."

Pinto went on to tell how he'd captured his first range pony, but he didn't quite get to the end.

"Here they are!" Alice Tubbs called as she swung the side door wide open and marched into the barn. "Just like I thought, Pa. Pinto's gabbin' away the mornin', keepin' the boys from their lessons and Muley there from his chores."

"I was workin' de roan's sore tendon," Pinto countered. "As to dem boys, I never got myself paid to boss dem. Thad'd be yer natural born pleasure, wouldn't it be, Alice?"

The boys chuckled at their red-faced sister, but it didn't last. Elroy Tubbs waved them outside, then propped a foot onto an anvil and stared at Pinto Lowery.

"Know it's in your nature to spin yarns, Lowery, but I won't have you philosophizin' when work's waitin' to get done," Tubbs complained. "Bad enough Muley's lazy. Don't need Tom and Ted turnin' out that way."

"I work hard enough," Muley objected.

"Hush," Pinto said, motioning Muley to silence. "Was jus' de boy in 'em comin' out, Mr. Tubbs. Youngsters never have much patience waitin' fer wagons and such. As for de tale, it wasn't one thad'd do 'em harm."

"It wastes their time," Tubbs argued.

"Well, some boys burn down barns smokin' cigars. I never heard a story to hurt anybody. I'll hurry 'em along from now on, though. Yer de boss, and you call de tune."

"It's just you have 'em dreamin' about chasin' horses and huntin' buffalo," Tubbs explained. "That'd turn any farmboy's head."

"Guess you're right," Pinto confessed. "I don't know much, I guess. Do have a knack for drawin' wild cridders, though. Horses and boy children mainly."

"Well, you do your work," Tubbs said begrudgingly. "Better hurry it up, too. Saw some dust on the Weatherford road. I'd guess the freight wagons are early."

"Den I'd bes' lead out de horses," Pinto said, giving the roan a final touch of salve. "Won't be a minute."

"Better not," Tubbs replied. "I hear horses now."

"What's due?" Muley asked as he trotted over and opened the first stall. Is it two or three? I can't ever remember."

"Three wagons," Pinto answered. "So you see, we won't need that pacer. He wouldn't care to heave that load."

Muley gazed at the sleek horse and covered his face. In another moment the correct animals were paired. Pinto left Muley to watch the team and walked out to supervise the freight unloading. But the expected wagons were nowhere to be found.

"Where are they?" Pinto called.

"Wasn't wagons at all," Tom said, hurrying over. "Just riders. Pa took them along inside with him. Most anyway. There's a couple o' young ones got left outside. Likely their pa don't trust 'em inside."

"Could be," Pinto said, following Tom to where three slight-shouldered young men tended half a dozen horses. One was filling a cigarette paper with tobacco. The other two were seeing their horses got fresh water.

"Why don't you take 'em a dipper from de well?" Pinto suggested as he waved to the three young visitors. "But afterward you trot along to de barn and climb up to de loft, hear?"

"What?" Tom asked.

"Take Ted and Alice along if you happen across 'em."

"Pinto?"

"Don't ask me questions, Tommy. I got no time nor answers either. Hurry along wid you."

The twelve-year-old stepped to the well, drew a dipper of cool water from the bucket, and set off toward the strangers. Pinto walked past the trio and stepped inside the freight company office.

"Here's another one now," a dark-haired man in his early twenties called.

"It's my stablehand," Tubbs explained as he glanced anxiously at Pinto. "Does some smithin', too. Maybe he could have a look at your horses and tell you what ails 'em."

"Yeah, Joe, bet he can," the youngish fellow said, turning to a tall, heavyset man with a nose someone had spread over half his face.

"It's a beauty, ain't it?" the big man asked Pinto. "Little boy there took to it right off, didn't you, son?"

Ted Tubbs nodded his head and hugged his father's leg.

"Got it busted three times," the younger visitor explained. "Once in a fist fight, once by a pine log, and the last time by a Jacksboro deputy."

"Won't that deputy bother anybody else," Joe said, pounding a big fist against the wall. "Will he, Pat?"

"Not 'less he comes back as a ghost," the younger man said, laughing. "Now, Mr. Tubbs, why don't you tell us 'bout them wagons?"

"Jus' whad's . . ." Pinto started to object.

"Hush, Lowery!" Tubbs shouted. "Look around you. Can't you see what's happened?"

Pinto stared grimly around the room. Faye Tubbs stood anxiously with Alice in one corner. Elroy and Ted faced the big man with the broken nose. Pat, the younger one, kept vigil over the door. The shotgun that normally stood in the gun rack beside the desk was gone, as were the three Winchester rifles. Pat drew a pocket Colt from his right pocket. Big Joe didn't seem to need a gun.

"Who's outside now?" Joe asked. Pat stepped outside and began a short tour of the Tubbs place. He was gone maybe ten minutes. When he returned, Joe repeated his earlier question.

"Was a boy passin' a dipper o' water about," Pat explained. "He seems to've gone."

"Neighbor boy," Pinto broke in. He flashed a warning with his eyes, and the Tubbses remained silent. "I asked him to tend yer men," Pinto went on to say. "Then he was hurryin' along to school."

"Anybody else here?" Joe demanded.

"That's all," Tubbs replied.

"You're a liar, mister!" Pat shouted, striking Tubbs with the back on his hand. As Tubbs collapsed onto the floor, Pat laughed. "Was a boy in the barn."

Pinto started to speak, but Pat jabbed the pistol into his ribs.

"Don't get yourself all riled, mister. We don't aim to hurt anybody. Just come for the money."

"What money?" Pinto cried. "All we do here's ship goods on de marked road."

"That right?" Joe asked. "Or is it what ole Tubbs here tells you? Why, he looks to keep you at starvin' wages, friend. Past three months this fellow's been shippin' gold and silver for the carpetbaggin' Yanks in Jacksboro. Tax money. Sends it down to Austin in tool crates. How's that for clever?"

"Not clever enough," Pat observed. "We Hannigans got eyes."

"Yer Joe Hannigan?" Pinto asked, feeling his toes grow numb.

"Heard o' me, have you? More reason to do what you're told. I don't make war on Texans if I can help it. Just on gold boxes and cash drawers. Open up that 'un yonder."

Tubbs complied with his orders, and Pinto took charge of Ted for a moment. The youngster felt feverish to the touch, and he was clearly worried. Tubbs and the women were even worse. There was a trace of murder in the eyes of Big Nose Joe Hannigan. Pinto knew enough about the outlaw to judge that killing the whole population of Hill Junction wouldn't rob Hannigan of much sleep.

Once the cash drawer was emptied, Joe sent his brother Pat out to tie the money behind a packhorse. A bit later the freight wagons rolled in. The drivers surrendered without a shot, and the outlaws quickly ransacked the supplies.

"Here's the gold, Joe!" one of the young thieves announced. "Now what do we do with the people?"

"I could take 'em to the barn," Pat suggested with a cruel grin. Only now did Pinto take note of something thin and shiny popping out of Pat's pocket. Muley's mouth organ! There was blood on Pat's boots, too, and . . .

"Muley!" Pinto shouted, leaping past the Hannigans and starting toward the barn. An outlaw rushed over and blocked the path. A second raider slammed a forearm into Pinto's ribs, doubling him over. Before Pinto could catch his breath, Pat appeared, pistol in hand.

"Ever hear this tune, Patches?" Pat asked, pressing the mouth organ against his lips and playing a jaunty version of "Dixie". "Now you be real good, mister, and maybe my big brother'll let you get a little bit older."

"Thad boy was simple," Pinto growled. "Never would've caused you a particle o' trouble."

"Wouldn't let go o' the mouth organ," Pat explained, drawing out his knife. "So I gutted him like a catfish."

"Dear Lord," Faye Tubbs whimpered as the outlaws dragged her outside. Big Nose Joe held a knife against fifteen-year-old Alice's throat.

"You've got your money!" Tubbs shouted as he struggled to free himself from the grasp of a young outlaw. "And you've killed!"

"Maybe we'll kill somebody else," Pat suggested. "Or maybe pleasure ourselves a hair."

Pat stepped toward Alice, and little Ted raced over.

"Ma!" the terrified boy screamed.

"I'll tend him," Pat said, turning that way.

"Stop, Teddy!" Faye pleaded as she reached for the boy. "Ted!"

Pat leveled his Colt and fired a single bullet into the ten-year-old's hip. Ted fell in a heap, and Pat holstered his pistol.

"Murderer!" Alice screamed.

"My Colt's got a lot o' use left in it," Pat replied, turning toward the girl. "We got time, Joe?"

"Best we move on along," Big Nose Joe answered. "Burn the wagons and what supplies we don't take with us. Run the horses away. Be sure they got no guns. Wouldn't want any vengeful papas on my trail."

"There's a better way to make sure o' that," Pat said, drawing the Colt.

"Boy's got a taste for killin', don't he?" Joe asked, slapping his brother to the ground. "I got no love o' posses, little brother. You go murderin' little kids and such, people take note. There's neighbors already growin' curious, what with you shootin' off your gun. Now get onto a horse and let's leave this place behind us. I got the itch to ride."

Pinto rushed over to where Faye was tending little Ted. The child was a lump of shudders. His face was already paling, and blood stained his trouser leg, collecting in a pool on the dusty ground.

"Give me a try, ma'am," Pinto said, taking cloth strips torn from Faye Tubbs's petticoats and binding the bloody wound. "Had practice at such, you see."

"I've heard stories," the woman said, fighting to regain her composure. It wasn't easy. Already the odor of burning wagons filled the air, and smoke blended with the gray morning to obscure the horizon.

"Look after him good, Lowery," Elmer pleaded, sitting beside his son with a face paled by shock and fear.

"He won't die, will he?" Alice asked.

"Where's Tom?" her mother added.

"Safe, I pray," Pinto muttered as he glanced at the barn. The outlaws were driving the last of the horses out toward the open range. As they left, Pinto recalled Big Nose Joe Hannigan's words.

I know all about de itch to ride, Pinto thought as he spat dust from his mouth. He had the urge to be anywhere else than the Tubbs place at that moment. Anywhere else!

Chapter 2

Pinto discovered Tom Tubbs cowering in a corner of the barn. The boy gazed anxiously toward where Muley Bryant lay facedown just inside the door, and Pinto nodded with understanding.

"Dey had no call to do that," the mustanger said as he helped Tom rise. "Nor to raid yer pa, neither."

"Nor to shoot Teddy," Tom mumbled as they reached the door.

"Hoped you didn't know 'bout that," Pinto said, shaking his head.

"Saw most of it," Tom explained. "Guess you know they might have kilt me if I'd stayed out there."

"Didn't shoot me," Pinto pointed out. "Weren't altogether hard o' heart. Let yer ma and Alice be. Was gold dey come fer."

"Sure," Tom grumbled. Then, when his mother spotted him, he raced to her side. The Tubbs family circled around Ted and offered comfort and encouragement. Pinto took note of that.

"You don't belong there, Pinto," he told himself. And he walked back to the barn to tend Muley.

By late afternoon little Ted was resting comfortably in his bed. A doctor had come out from Cleburne to dig the bullet from the youngster's hip, and what fever had ensued broke an hour later.

"Thank God for that," his mother had proclaimed.

Elroy Tubbs, meanwhile, had collected a group of neighbors, chased down his horses, and was readying himself to set out after the outlaws. The posse showed little enthusiasm for the task ahead, though. They had no hunger for an ambush.

Fool's errand, Pinto thought. Big Nose Joe Hannigan and his outfit weren't going to be brought to bay by a band of shotgun-wielding farmers and shopkeepers.

As for the Hood County sheriff, Murray Ralls, he contented himself with sending telegrams.

"Let them politicians in Jacksboro worry themselves sick over that gold," Ralls told Tubbs. "Ain't a penny of it mine."

Tubbs was visibly disappointed when Pinto refused to join the posse.

"I expected loyalty from you, Lowery," the freighter complained. "And after all, they were none too friendly toward you."

"Somebody ought to tend Muley," Pinto argued. "He got killed, remember?"

"Wrap him in a blanket and dig him a hole," Tubbs suggested. "We can't do him any good now. Better to punish the ones who killed him."

"Wasn't but a boy, and a simple one at thad," Jonas Birney, one of the neighbors, agreed.

"Maybe," Pinto admitted. "Still, he ought to be cleaned up respectable. A proper place should be dug, with a marker put up. We should get a preacher to read words over him. If he's got family . . ."

"He doesn't," Tubbs said, spitting as he slung a saddle onto the back of broad-backed brown stallion. "There'll be no crowd of mourners, either. Now come along."

"Might be he'll have jus' one soul at his buryin'," Pinto replied. "Me! He'll have thad one, though. Muley never dealed me false, nor gave me call to doubt him. I'll see right done him."

"You may just do it jobless!" Tubbs hollered. "Let's go, men. Lowery wouldn't be any use in a fight anyway."

Pinto glared as the riders set off northward. *What would Elmer Tubbs know o' fightin'?* he wondered.

Actually there wasn't much to tending Muley. The poor boy was hardly marked. Except for the hole in his chest, it looked like he was sleeping. Oh, there was the blood, sure, but it was washed off easily enough.

Not all the Tubbses shared Elmer's disdain for the slain stableboy. Tom offered a clean shirt, and Alice supplied an old pair of her father's shoes. Muley had decent enough trousers set aside for rare ventures into Cleburne for church. Pinto provided stockings and a string tie from his own scant belongings.

"Wish I could put yer mouth organ in here with you," Pinto lamented as he and Faye wrapped Muley in a time-worn quilt. "But I guess dey'll give you a harp to play up yonder."

"Sure, they will," Tom said by way of comfort.

Pinto dug the grave alone. He found a spot half a mile up the road where a clump of willows crowded a spring. Even on that gray February afternoon the place seemed halfway cheerful.

"It'll do," he announced as he struck a spade into the hard ground. "And come spring dere'll be flowers."

It was young Tom who nailed a pair of white pickets into a cross and inscribed Muley's name in carefully drawn letters.

Martin Bryant, horse lover, Tom had thought to write.

"Never knew he had a proper name," Pinto said as he eased the body to its resting place.

"Everybody's got a proper name," Alice declared. "Or did have. Muley told me his last Christmas when we had that barn dance. He was all elbows and knees mostly, but he never did anybody harm."

Pinto began the brief memorial by reading from a battered Bible. He'd barely begun when Faye Tubbs rode up atop a wagon. In the bed little Ted looked out, pale and battered but alert.

"He oughtn't to've lef' his bed," Pinto grumbled.

"Muley was my friend, too," Ted argued. "I had to come say good-bye."

The words spoke for the whole company, and Pinto said as much. He then read two short passages, and Faye added a fourth from memory.

"Rest easy, Muley," Tom said when Pinto announced it was time to fill in the grave.

"No more hogs to feed," Alice whispered.

"You'll break some hearts up there," Faye added as she draped an arm over Alice's shoulders. "And chase some good horses, I'm certain."

"Be lonely on de Llano," Pinto said last of all. The others climbed into the wagon, and Faye drove them home. Pinto stayed and shoveled earth over his young friend. It wasn't the first time he'd buried a comrade. At least this time there'd been time to wash away the blood and see a proper hole was dug. Just the same, death had a way of leaving a man cold and hollow when it passed close by. Pinto Lowery hoped to give the grim reaper a wide berth for a time.

Elmer Tubbs returned near dusk the day after the burial. The freighter said little. He was trail-worn and dust-choked. After embracing his wife and looking in on Ted, he marched to the barn.

Pinto was looking after Tubbs's weary horse at that moment.

"Well, at least you've put yourself to some use," Tubbs grumbled. "Come dawn have me a fresh mount saddled. Ready one for yourself as well. You ride tomorrow, either with me or on your own."

"Was only waitin' fer you to get back," Pinto answered, motioning to where his two horses stood ready for hard travel. He'd rolled his belongings in a blanket and tied them atop the pack horse.

"Be some winter left," Tubbs growled, twirling a watch fob. "You'll wish you'd decided elsewise."

"Likely," Pinto replied. "Wouldn't be de firs' mistake I made. Still, I can't work for a man's got no time to honor his dead. And if I did, I'd have to think hard on stayin' with anyone fool enough to hunt dem Hannigans. Thad's fer de law, or maybe de army. Yer sure to come to grief on dem men's trail."

"You said your piece. Now get along with you!"

"I got good-byes to make," Pinto said as he led the horse to an empty stall. "And dere's wages I'm owed."

"Well, you don't expect me to have money for wages after yesterday!" Tubbs yelled. "And for a coward!"

"Mister Tubbs, I'd watch my words," Pinto said, slapping the horse into its stall and turning red-faced toward the freighter. "I'm owed money, but I can take thad in trade. Thad little chessnut mare'll square us. You write out a bill 'o sale. As to what you jus' said, you repeat it and I'll give you a nose to match Joe Hannigan's. Yer enditled to your opinions, but no man thad stayed at his fire when I was freezin' my toes off at Petersburg's fit to judge honor nor duty. Not by my way o' thinkin'. You want yerself a fight, I'll oblige!"

Pinto strode up to Elmer Tubbs so that their chins near touched. Fury darkened the mustanger's brow, and Tubbs gave way.

"Thought not," Pinto muttered as he walked past Tubbs and hurried along to the house. It took but half an hour to bid Alice and the boys farewell. He swapped a few words with Faye as well, but he wouldn't answer her questions.

"With Elmer off chasing those Hannigans, I'd feel safer if you stayed," she told him. "What's got you in such a hurry to ride?"

"I won't speak ill of a man in his own house," Pinto finally told her. "You'll have to trus' me do have my reasons."

Pinto then stepped onto the porch and located Elmer Tubbs.

"Here's your bill of sale, Lowery," the freighter announced. "Now you know the road west, I believe."

"Sure do," Pinto said, accepting the paper. He then walked to the corral and threw a rope over the chestnut's neck. Pinto wasted not a moment in leading the animal to the barn. There he climbed onto a spotted mustang, tied off the pack horse and the chestnut to his saddlehorn, and started west.

By daybreak Pinto had passed through Cleburne and was winding his way north into the wild Brazos country. The Brazos had a way of running swift and wide in late winter and early spring, and he had the devil's own luck finding a reliable ford. Only when he and his horses were across on the north bank did he feel he'd finally escaped the confinement of the Tubbs place. And even then he hadn't eluded the haunting emptiness that had filled Muley's stone-cold eyes.

"Boy never had a chance," Pinto muttered as he halted along the river. "But den we don't any o' us have much o' one."

Tired and wracked with hunger, Pinto hobbled his horses and left them to graze atop a nearby hill. He dangled a baited hook in the shallows and snared a fat river-catfish. In no time he'd built up a fire, skinned and gutted the fish, and was enjoying a breakfast of sorts beneath the early morning sun.

There was something cheering about daylight. It chased off the gray February mists and brought a warming glow to the land. That particular morning it put Pinto in mind of morning chores, though, of Muley grumbling about hog slop and horse dung.

Pinto finished off the catfish and sighed. He then walked to the packhorse, untied a blanket, and rolled it out onto a clover-covered slope. After kicking off his boots and loosening his belt, he sprawled on the blanket and let sleep whirl him away from his grief.

It didn't entirely work. For a time Pinto did drift through a world of fluffy clouds and sweet silence. Then he found himself crawling through the rock-strewn Pennsylvania hell to the south of Gettysburg. The whole of the Marshall Guards, or at least what was left of the company after Sharpsburg and Chancellorsville, was creeping through the Devil's Den, exchanging long-range rifle shots with Yankee sharpshooters.

Minie balls stung the rocks, sending deadly splinters of lead and stone into many a man. George Lowery had hesitated before continuing.

"What you feared of, Georgie?" Jamie Haskell had called as he rushed forward. "Cain't them Yanks kill you but once."

"Jamie!" Pinto had cried, leaping toward his foolhardy friend. The two of them got to within a hundred yards of Little Round Top when a pair of cannons fired from the hilltop. A giant boulder up ahead simply disintegrated. Smoke and powder blinded the charging Confederates. Pinto never saw the steel fragment that took Jamie's legs. He himself was thrown back against a fallen tree with such force that a bone in his leg snapped.

"Move along, Lowery!" the captain urged as he waved his sword overhead. "We close to got 'em."

"No, they got us," Jamie called, grinning as he sat in a sea of his own blood.

"Fool boy," Pinto had scolded as he dragged himself to his friend's aid. "Done it dis time!"

"Yup," Jamie said, staring down at the stubs attached to his lacerated waist. "You'll write my mama."

"Lord, Jamie, you know I will," Pinto had gasped as he fought to collect his wits. "I'll tie off de stubs and . . ."

"Fool's errand," young Haskell had announced. "I'm plum blown in half, George Lowery. Teach me to run ahead like a peach-fuzzed kid!"

Pinto recalled laughing. They didn't sport a dozen chin whiskers between them that summer of 1863. Barely nineteen. It had seemed old enough. Now it was painfully young. But for Jamie Haskell, it was as old as he'd ever get.

George Lowery had stayed with his friend in spite of a fierce artillery exchange around noon. By then Jamie had bled out his life, but Pinto had been reluctant to leave.

"It's time, Lowery," the captain had finally commanded. "Come on. I'll help you along. You need some tendin' your own self."

"Wait fer me to bury Jamie," Pinto had objected.

"Yanks'll do it," the captain argued. "We don't get movin' they might just have to bury us, too."

Pinto was determined to stay, but Merritt Hardy and Ben Turley arrived. They were tall, lean, and farmboy strong.

"Ain't leavin' but one friend behind here," Hardy declared as he handed over his rifle and picked up Pinto bodily. "Cap'n, you write ole Jamie's name on him, hear? Only right those Yanks know what kind o' man they gone and kilt."

The captain had scrawled Jamie's name in his order book, then had torn out the page and tucked it into the boyish-looking corpse's pocket.

"Now get along with you!" the captain ordered as a fresh round of artillery fire began. Hardy struggled through the rocky ravine, carrying a pain-tortured George Lowery along as Turley and the captain followed.

Pinto soon found himself sailing across the battlefield, soaring over the bloodstained wheatfields and orchards of Gettysburg. Later he found himself in a barn with his leg braced by a pair of oak splints. Only a threat from Ben Turley had prevented a harried doctor from cutting that leg off.

"Best to lose a limb than your life," the doc had argued.

"One-legged man's little use to Bob Lee and even less on the Texas plain," Turley'd replied. "Now tend the break well as you can. Then I'll take over. I got five brothers and two sisters back home in Jefferson, and there's not a one of 'em's not broke somethin' or another."

Many a man died from amputation. Ben Turley surely saved Pinto's life. But that only came after a world of pain and fever passed.

There were men who might have returned to Texas with a lamed leg, but George Lowery fought on. He survived the confusion of the Wilderness when the First Texas threatened to mutiny if General Lee didn't leave the front line. Then, at Spotsylvania Court House, he helped bury Ben Turley. Merritt Hardy froze in the Petersburg trenches in November of 1864. In fact, only nine of the original

Marshall Guards lived to lay down a rifle at Appomattox.

As the nightmare continued, faces of slain friends and murdered enemies appeared like phantoms in Pinto's mind. He shook violently and flayed his hands at his sides. Scenes too horrible to describe tormented him.

"War's not the frolic we thought, eh?" legless Jamie whispered.

"Should've ducked that last volley," Ben Turley spoke. His mutilated face sent daggers of pain twisting and turning through Pinto's insides.

Finally Muley flashed his easy grin and spoke of the high times they would share chasing down range ponies.

"No!" Pinto screamed as he bolted awake. He shuddered as he felt the damp sweat which soaked every inch of him.

"We'll have a time or two, won't we?" Muley's ghostlike voice seemed to whisper.

"No, dis year it'll jus' be me," Pinto replied. "Jus' me and a thousand ghosts of men better'n I'll ever be."

He blinked the exhaustion from his eyes and stared at the yellow sun high overhead. It was near noon, maybe a hair past. He'd slept hours, or had his eyes closed, anyway. He hadn't had much rest, what with the nightmare and all.

Always thought it was not buryin' Jamie brought on his ghos', Pinto mused. *Now it seems buryin' a man's bones ain't all you do to hush his ghos'*.

No, some things just weren't to be set aside. Many would be with a man for all his days. Ever since Gettysburg George Lowery had blamed himself for not seeing Jamie to cover. After all, they were as close as brothers, the two of them. And now there'd been Muley. That sliver of a boy didn't have the smarts to hide from a fight. No, it was Pinto who should've seen Muley to safety before setting off to the freight office.

"Man's got just a few chances in his life to stand tall," old Grandpa Lowery had once said. The old man had done his standing at San Jacinto and again fighting the Mexicans with Winfield Scott.

"I had my chances, too," Pinto remarked as he rolled up his blanket and tied it atop the packhorse. "But I never been as strong as what was needed. And men've died on account o' thad!"

Pinto Lowery was thinking that over as he removed the hobbles from his horses and climbed atop the mustang. *Maybe nex' time'll be different*. Deep down Pinto hoped there wouldn't be a next time. And all along he knew there would be.

Chapter 3

It was strange how memories that should have died at Appomattox eight long years before should have haunted Pinto Lowery so. For three days the nightmare faces of fallen comrades visited his dreams. As he wandered across the wind-swept range, passing scattered clusters of grazing longhorns and the crude picket ranch houses of their owners, he couldn't help recalling old dreams born on the trail to Kansas.

"I'll have myself a herd one day," Ken Preston had boasted. "How 'bout yourself, Pinto?"

"Oh, wouldn't be so mad," a younger Lowery had confessed. "But mos'ly I'd like to run myself some horses."

Dreams had their way of coming back at a man, didn't they? Here Ken got himself pistol shot in Wichita by some Kansas farmer over a bit of foolishness with his daughter, and Pinto had passed too many winters mending harnesses and loading freight. Finally he was back on the Llano, sniffing out ponies.

It was late on the glorious first afternoon of March 1873, when Pinto Lowery at last came upon the unshod tracks of a mustang herd. He smelled traces of the animals before that, and for twenty miles he'd spotted their dung amidst the sea of yellow buffalo grass.

As he stalked the horses, he put aside those lingering memories of an unfulfilled past.

"I was born to hunt horses," he announced to the world. "Ain't a man in Texas does it half so good, and none at all more inclined to de trade."

Pinto urged his horse onward. He rode only three or four miles before locating the distinctive mottled colorings of a range pony. Beyond the first animal another two dozen grazed. At Pinto's approach, the horses lifted their nostrils to the wind. But days on the trail had blended Pinto's natural odors with those of horse sweat and damp ground. The animals noted nothing peculiar and relaxed their guard.

Pinto, meanwhile, led his packhorse and the chestnut mare through a narrow ravine and along to a low hill overlooking the Brazos. A spattering of willows lined the river there, affording good firewood. It made for an ideal camping spot, and Pinto wasted no time in hobbling his horses and unpacking his belongings. It was only later, when the midday sun sent the horses to the river for a drink, that Pinto counted them and made plans for their capture. Of the thirty-six animals he counted, he hoped to snare half to two-thirds.

"How exactly do you plan to capture two dozen horses single-handed?" Bob Toney, another veteran of the First Texas and a prominent Parker County rancher, had asked two summers before when Pinto had announced a like intent.

"Oh, catchin' 'em's no trouble," Pinto had answered then. "It's keepin' 'em's de trick."

So it was now.

To begin with, Pinto had learned long ago even a dozen men had little hope of roping more than five or six horses once the herd took to flight. If a man was just after a saddle mount, a rope would get him there. But if he was after a profit, he needed to have the horses do most of the work.

Pinto knew once the animals stampeded, a leader would emerge. It wasn't hard to spot which one. The strongest of the stallions gathered around himself a harem of sorts. Oh, he'd sometimes tolerate another stallion or even three or four if the herd was large enough. Mostly the leader drove his rivals off, even those he himself had sired. There were always colts about, though.

The leader of the current herd was a tall, prancing black with a splash of white across his face. It seemed likely he was the offspring of some rancher's mare mated with a mustang. Or maybe the horse had been stolen by Comanches as a colt. The black was half a hand taller than his companions, and he tirelessly worked his way among the harem as if to tell the three other younger and smaller stallions that they had best keep their place.

"Horse like that 'un's sure to leap a four foot fence," Pinto told himself. "Well, I'll build mine six."

As for where, Pinto followed the ravine into a walled canyon. Where once a creekbed had promised freedom on the opposite side, a massive rock slide now barred the way. It was a perfect box.

Pinto set to felling live oaks. In two days' time he'd cut posts and planted them in the rocky ground. Rails six feet high followed. He left a narrow entrance eight feet wide so the animals could get inside the canyon. It wouldn't take much to slide rails into place afterward, trapping the whole herd.

"Well, dere you are," Pinto announced when he finally finished the back-breaking work. "As good as a work corral!"

Now all he had to do was coax the horses into the ravine and run them down the canyon. *All*? Pinto asked himself. It was enough.

"It'll either work or it won't," he mumbled as he climbed atop his spotted mustang and headed toward where he'd last seen the range ponies grazing. He slipped up on the rear of the herd quietly, then exploded into action. Howling like a banshee, he waved a blanket overhead and fired off three chambers of his battered old Navy Colt. The noise echoed across the far hills, giving the desired effect of driving the horses away from the river and down the narrow ravine. In no time at all the animals pressed together in a knot. Their big leader fought to take control, but Pinto refused to give pause. As he screamed and waved the blanket, the mustangs hurled themselves deeper and deeper down the ravine. Amidst the dust and confusion, the defiant stallion was driven along toward the confines of the canyon.

Oh, one or two colts did break away. Being swift and nimble, they were better suited to climbing the walls of the ravine. But once the walls became rockier and steeper, escape was no longer possible. The frightened animals lumbered onward, unaware that they were hurrying toward captivity.

In half an hour's time it was all over. The last of the ponies squeezed through the gap in Pinto's fence and rushed toward the blocked exit. Two horses tried to scale the rock slide, but neither succeeded. Meanwhile, Pinto slid the hidden rails into place, completing the rock and wood corral.

"Now I got you, boy," Pinto shouted to the big stallion. "Tomorrow we get on with de breakin'."

The big black screamed defiance. He charged around the canyon, trying every possible means of escape. Finally he trotted over and tackled the fence. Even his heavy hooves couldn't dislodge those posts and rails, though.

"I build a thing to stay," Pinto called to the stallion. "Bes' you understand it. These others'll make good work ponies. You'll carry me 'cross de Llano!"

The stallion reared up and cried out stubbornly. He then turned and kicked as the fence with his hind legs. Finally he raced at a gallop and threw himself at the wall. It didn't budge, though, and the horse bounced backward in a swirl of dust.

"Bus' dem ribs, and you'll be crowbait!" Pinto yelled.

The horse paid him little mind, though. But by the time dusk fell, the big black had begun to realize the futility of escape.

Pinto Lowery devoted two and a half months to the mustangs. By that time twenty-seven of the beasts begrudgingly accepted a bit and tolerated a rider. Of course the rider was George Lowery.

And there was some question as to whether the white-faced black stallion did either.

"Every time up's a puzzle, eh, boy?" Pinto asked as he mounted the defiant stallion one mid-May morning. "You jus' can't give yerself over, can you?"

As if to answer, the stallion shook his head and bucked a moment before Pinto squeezed the rebellion out of the beast with his knees.

"Let's take a bit of a ride," Pinto suggested.

He then trotted toward the fence, dismounted long enough to slide back two rails, and led the horse through. After replacing the rails, Pinto approached the stallion cautiously. Never before had he dared take the horse out into the ravine. As for the stallion, the animal gave a snort and dipped his head. Then it waited meekly for Pinto to climb atop.

"Thought you'd skedaddle sure," Pinto remarked as he urged the stallion into a trot. "Nothin' holdin' you, but o' course you didn't know."

The stallion responded by rearing up on his hind legs and then setting off down the ravine quick as lightning. The horse was a comet—all speed and fury. Pinto hung onto the reins and shouted encouragement.

"Go, won't you? Show me what you can manage!"

The animal raced down the ravine, splashed across the Brazos shallows, and galloped on toward the boundless plain. For a time Pinto gave the horse its head. Only later did he turn the stallion west and then north—back to the canyon.

"Yer a regular dancer!" Pinto exclaimed upon returning. The mares stirred anxiously as the lathered stallion pranced through the open gate. But Pinto had no trouble sliding the rails back into place, and when he removed the saddle and drew out the bit, the big horse dropped its head onto Pinto's shoulder. The mustanger stroked the animal and sighed.

"Done stole de wind from you, boy," Pinto remarked. "Ain't wild no more. But you's as good a pony as a man's got a right to dream 'bout. Time we took ourselves a ride toward town, sold off a few o' dese others."

Pinto slept long and well that night. His dreams filled with the cries of auctioneers as cattlemen gathered to bid up the price of Pinto Lowery's prime cow ponies.

"They's jest mustangs," one young cowboy declared.

"You ain't been alive long enough to know what a good horse is, boy!" another chastised. "Lowery was runnin' ponies down when you was wettin' yerself."

Stacks of banknotes and fistfuls of gold pieces reduced the herd. That money spelled a prosperous future. Land was cheap, and a few thousand dollars could buy a fine stretch of country. Hadn't men turned the profits from driving mavericks to Kansas into empires? Bob Toney had started the Lazy T with gold pieces earned from selling the Yank cavalry a batch of remounts.

Soon the vision of a wealthy and respected Pinto Lowery appeared. Bankers tipped their hats, and ladies curtsied. His credit was good in every saloon west of Fort Worth. Then a big-nosed monster appeared, smoking pistol in hand, and stole it all away.

"Got unfinished business," Joe Hannigan insisted as he nodded to his brother Pat. The younger Hannigan drew out Muley's mouth organ and struck up a tune. The first notes of "Dixie" were tormenting Pinto when he suddenly bolted upright. The dream exploded, leaving only bits of nightmare to haunt the nervous mustanger.

"Lord, thad was a turn," Pinto said, mopping his damp brow and fighting to regain control of his heaving chest. "Poor time fer de bad dreams to come back."

He steadied his nerves and glanced around at the horses. They were calm enough, and he tried to put aside the vision of Joe Hannigan's cruel eyes. The memory of Muley's pale face was heavy in Pinto's thoughts just then, though, and it was a time yet before he could get back to sleep.

"Hard life, ridin' de Llano alone," Pinto remarked as a rare May chill bit into his back. He recalled the bantering of the Tubbs boys,

Alice's good-natured nagging, Muley's fool stunts and addled thinking. There was comfort to hearing them climbing the loft on winter mornings. He missed Faye's cooking, too.

He didn't miss the violent morning that had taken Muley Bryant's young life. Nor did he yen for one of Elmer's tongue-lashings.

"Oh, well," Pinto muttered. "Life's a trade. It's jus' a matter o' swappin' one thing fer another. Sometimes you do jus' fine. Others you wind up with de short stick."

It was a philosophy of sorts. Pinto Lowery believed it with all his being.

Come morning, Pinto set to work assembling a sample herd. He lined up ten of the fittest mares, together with one young stallion. As for himself, he planned to ride the big black. He felt a sort of kinship for the beast, and he hoped to give the animal a real test on the twenty-five-mile ride to the Lazy T. If the horses didn't sell to Bob Toney, then Pinto would take them into the market town of Defiance.

Actually, he wasn't too worried. Soon the northern Texas herds would start north toward Kansas. Cowboys were always in woeful need of saddle mounts, and a Lowery pony brought top price.

"You others stay put," Pinto said as he led his string of eleven through the gate and slid the rails back into place. Some men might have taken the lot. Pinto took what he could control. Then, too, why flood the market? The others would sell easily enough, but maybe not at top dollar. This way men hard up for a horse would bid an animal's worth.

He led his four-hoof procession out of the ravine and up to the banks of the river. Soon they were snaking their way eastward toward the Lazy T. Since most of the region's ranches spread out north and south of the river, Pinto soon swung north to avoid crossing the land of men he didn't know. It had been two years since he last rode that country, and a lot could happen in two days on the Texas frontier. Then, too, the river wound through the Palo Pinto Mountains in twists and turns that would vex a man in a hurry. Pinto didn't much bother about timepieces or seasons, but it was a matter of some importance to visit buyers before they were all heading north to Kansas.

He judged to have crossed into Wise County late that afternoon. The country didn't much change, but the character of the dwellings did. Out Palo Pinto way the Indians had held back settlement considerably, and more than one town or ranch got itself depopulated when raiding season came around. But just as Pinto began to breathe a hair easier, he spotted a sea of eerie white bones just ahead.

"Buffs," he said, steadying his hold on the black. "Hunters done it, boy. Murdered a whole world of 'em here. Comanche kids gone hungry 'cause of it, I'd bet."

As if the mention of their name conjured them magically into being, three bare-chested youngsters with painted faces suddenly appeared on the far hillside.

"Now dere's luck!" Pinto muttered as he turned to the right toward a distant oak-studded hillside. "Isn't that jus' like it is, boy? Soon's you got somethin', 'nother comes along to take it away!"

The young Indians noticed at once. They didn't shout or charge, though. Instead they rode parallel, halting only when it appeared Pinto might make a stand on the hillside.

"Get clear o' here!" a rifle-toting farmer shouted when Pinto tried to find some shelter. "You'll bring dem injuns down on us, sure's day."

Pinto gazed at a wagon half-hidden in the trees. Seven youngsters peered out from behind furniture stacked in the wagon's bed or from around wheels or horses. The eldest was a snip of a girl. Alongside her was a boy who might have been Muley Bryant's shaggy-haired younger brother.

"Yer safe," Pinto announced. "But I'd head west and down to de river soon's dem scouts clear you. Be a raidin' party close, I'd guess, and dem trees won't save yer hides if dey attack."

There was a hint of thanks in the eyes of the youngsters, but Pinto paid them little mind. The only move left him was to ride like wildfire for Jarrell's Ford and get across the Brazos. The higher southern bank was a natural rampart from which a man with a good rifle stood half a chance. The horses would be safe there, too.

The scouts seemed to sense Pinto's notion, for one of them suddenly broke away and headed north.

"Gone to get de menfolk," Pinto muttered. He then drew out a Henry rifle from its saddle scabbard and let fly a round toward the two remaining scouts. The shot unsettled the black, but it scattered the young Indians like seed corn at planting. "You nervous, are you?" Pinto yelled to the stallion. "Well, show 'em yer heels, boy! Let's go!"

He dropped the line holding the other horses as the black raced for the river. It wasn't needed. The horses were a herd again, and they followed the big black as before. The scouts, still shaken by the Henry's accurate fire, responded slowly. Pinto reached the river first, located the ford, and splashed onward to the far bank. He even managed to secure the precious horses before climbing onto the bank and waiting for the Indians.

"Comin'?" Pinto yelled. "Where'd you boys get do?"

The two scouts howled like wild men and plunged into the river. They weren't familiar with the swirls and bogs, though, and in short order both were unhorsed. They thrashed about for a moment before dragging themselves almost naked and weaponless to the near bank. Pinto waited in hopes they might turn away. They couldn't have been more than twelve—just children, really. But they recovered their bows quickly and sent arrows flying up the bank. Pinto ducked the first exchange and fired back. His first shot struck the left-handed scout in the shoulder and spun him around before depositing him in the shallows. Pinto fired a second time when the surviving scout charged. Only thirty feet separated them, and the Henry couldn't miss at that range. The bullet shattered the boy's elbow, but still he raced on. Another shot shattered the youngster's jaw and dropped him into the sand, writhing in pain.

"Fool!" Pinto said as he worked the Henry's lever and advanced a fresh shell into the firing chamber. "Jus' like Gettysburg. You cain't rush cannons, Jamie!"

A storm of riders then appeared at the river, led by a tall chief with all sorts of feathers tied in his hair. Pinto counted fifteen men, and he opened up on them immediately. The Comanches raised a shout and charged into the river. These newcomers weren't children, though, and the river didn't bother them anymore than a fly bothers a mountain. Pinto knocked one rider from a horse and fired on another. Then, as he tried to shift the lever, the rifle jammed.

"Now thad's a Henry fer you!" Pinto shouted as he pulled the old Navy Colt from his holster and prepared to make the Indians pay a price for his horses. The Comanches wailed and waved wicked-looking lances to unsettle his aim, but George Lowery had been in battles before. If the Army of the Potomac couldn't shake him loose from his hold on Petersburg, no batch of half-starved Comanches would move him now.

The first two Comanches started for Pinto, but neither got there. The Colt barked three times, and the two men stumbled back bleeding. *Only two shots left*, Pinto thought. *Well, there's the bowie knife.* It never came to that, however. The Comanches were shaken. They collected their wounded and turned away. Pinto made no move to stop them.

From the far bank of the river the tall chief hurled a torrent of abuse at Pinto Lowery. He pointed first to his chest and then to his back as if to tempt a shot. Finally the Indians bared themselves in contempt and screamed taunts.

"Go 'head and yell yer heart out, Comanch!" Pinto yelled back. "I done my speakin'," he added, waving the Colt.

As the Comanches slowly abandoned their hold on the river and retreated north, Pinto reloaded his pistol and began working on the jammed rifle. The third scout, the unhurt one, rode into the river and stood naked atop his pony, inviting a bullet to match those received by his companions. Here was the youngest of all, Pinto knew, sent back for help perhaps by an elder cousin or brother.

"Ain't there been enough hurt?" Pinto whispered to the wind. "Ain't a thousand dead buffs put their bones to dis place already?"

As if he heard the words, the young Comanche covered himself and slid back down onto the back of his horse. Riding away he sadly sang a warrior song.

Be dead inside a year, Pinto thought as he fought to erase the faces of the men he'd shot. *Starved or bluecoat shot, the bunch o' them!*

But George Lowery wouldn't be the one to have done it.

Pinto collected his wits and then gathered his horses. He was still ten miles from the Lazy T, and dusk was settling over the Llano.

Chapter 4

Pinto camped that night on a hillside overlooking the river. He could detect the small yellow-orange flames of campfires in the distance. Those would be roundup crews busy branding the yearlings and collecting a herd for the long trail north to Kansas. The dimmer pinpricks marked the windows of Bob Toney's ranchhouse. The place would be near deserted now, of course. Toney would have his best men on the range. That's where the work was to be found. Only the younger of his boys would remain at home with their mother.

From time to time the faint echoes of a cowboy ballad haunted the wind. Cowboys worked hard at roundup, and they ate more dust than beef or beans. Some had the poor luck to get themselves gored or trampled by one cantankerous longhorn or another. Others collapsed from the heat or went mad from the plagues of mosquitoes and horseflies that were never far from that army of hooves and tallow.

"Yup, was hard work," Pinto reminded himself. But as he hummed along with the eerie melodies, he recalled the odd sense of belonging that came with shared dangers, with putting your all into a task that needed doing. There were pranks, too—vexations the youngsters put upon their elders and double that many the veterans heaped upon the newcomers.

Pinto laughed as he recalled how young Jake Toney had convinced Abel Perkins tarantulas favored red flannel as nesting places. Poor Abel awoke one morning, hollering to high heaven as he jumped around shedding his long handles. Finally there stood Abel, stark naked, staring with relief at the twist of horse hair Jake had managed to slip beneath his drawers.

"Some spider, eh?" Jake called.

"Lord, boy, you did yourself a dance!" Bob added. "Lucky not to've caused your innards any harm!"

Pinto himself never much went in for pranking, but he had to admit that horse-hair spider trick brought the whole outfit to life. And he missed the tale-swapping and singing come nightfall that shook off the wearies left by trailing cattle.

"Got my own share o' dem wearies," Pinto muttered as he turned over on one side and closed his eyes. "Workin' cows up to Kansas wouldn't be so bad maybe."

No, and the wages earned at trail's end would merit the effort. Going north with Bob Toney flooded Pinto's mind with possibilities. Old Bob had been at Sharpsburg the day that minie ball tried to take off Pinto's left hand. And if not for taking fever, Bob would have been in the Devil's Den along with Jamie and the others.

"Be good to see an ole friend," Pinto said aloud. After all, there were pitiful few of them left.

He awoke to find a bright yellow sun filling the eastern sky. Down below, men drove cattle in bands of fifty or so in dust swirls that rose halfway to heaven. Pinto thought he recognized one or two of the cowboys. Surely that was little Ned Larsen there. Or one of Ned's brothers. Ned would be nigh on twenty now, and the slim-shouldered rider below couldn't be more than fifteen at full stretch.

Time passes, Pinto told himself as he pulled on his clothes and set about saddling the big black. He removed the hobbles from the horses next and led them down to the river. As the animals drank,

Pinto splashed water over his face and ran an old comb through his hair. Weeks on the Llano had made him a wild-eyed vagabond. A few minutes with a razor, though, cleared away most of the beard, and he buttoned up his shirt and added a black string tie. None of it improved the image grinning up at him from the surface of the river, though. "Can't make no Kentucky thoroughbred out o' some fool range pony," Pinto grumbled.

Once he was satisfied the horses had watered themselves, Pinto climbed atop the black stallion and drove the other ponies along ahead of him. There was no need to tie them now. The Lazy T wasn't a mile and a half away, and the mustangs wouldn't stray far from the black in any case. Only the painted stallion had even the slightest inclination toward roving, and Pinto took care to keep himself between the paint and freedom.

He rode past two roundup camps before reaching the ranchhouse. Pinto had half expected to locate Bob Toney at one or the other.

"He's back at the house, Pinto," Toney's brother Jake explained. "You'll find yourself welcome. The horses anyhow."

"Yeah?" Pinto called. "You found any horse-hair spiders among the youngsters o' late?"

"Oh, ever once in a while," Jake replied, laughing. "Biggest critters in Texas. Sure to end a cowboy's days, don't you know?"

"'Course dese men here know all 'bout that," Pinto said, eyeing the collection of scruffy teenagers that passed for a range crew. "None o' dem'd wear red flannel."

"What's red flannel got to do with spiders, mister?" a spindle-legged boy cried. "Ma swears by 'em."

"Got some myself," a second youngster added.

"Well, ole Jake'll tell you all 'boud it," Pinto said, exchanging a chuckle with young Toney. "You tell me how you do it dis time, won't you, Jake?"

"Sure, Pinto," Jake agreed. "Now get those horses along to Bob. He's sure to pay you top price for 'em."

Pinto paused a moment to study the nervous eyes of the cowboys. One was scratching his rump, and a second squirmed as Jake began his tale. Sure thing one of them would wind up with a knot of horse hair in his pants before morning.

Pinto laughed at the notion, then nudged the black into a trot. The other horses followed along, and soon the dozen animals and their wayfaring herder topped the low ridge that led to the Lazy T ranchhouse.

The sound of horses charging through the early morning mists was sufficient to rouse the occupants of the house. Bob Toney stumbled outside, shotgun in hand. He was joined shortly by a pair of bewildered stablehands. Ophelia Toney remained in the doorway with her three smallish sons.

"Mr. Toney, it's only horses," one of the hands observed.

"Not altogether," Toney observed, scratching his chin. "There's one no-account along!"

"Feared o' me, huh?" Pinto called as he turned the horses toward an empty corral. "You fire off that dere shotgun, you'll never catch a one o' dese ponies."

"Still, I might put a part in your hair, George Lowery! Might just be worth the loss."

"Whose loss?" Pinto exclaimed. "My horses. And my head, too."

Toney laughed as he set aside his shotgun. Pinto rolled off his saddle then, and the two old comrades clasped hands.

"You're about the last man I ever expected to happen by this morning," Toney declared. "Pinto. Was a wise man gave you that name, you old horse thief. Got a likely batch here. What'll you take for them?"

"A fair price," Pinto answered. "I'd get twenty-five from de army and fifty-five maybe if I drove 'em to de Colorado gold fields. Seein' you to be a friend and all, I'll turn 'em over fer forty."

"I bought my last saddle horse for thirty, and he was a stud that's brought me seven good colts so far."

"I've only got de one stallion, that paint dere, plus de mares. De black's gone and got my fancy."

"Worth the rest combined," Toney remarked. "Still, I'll take the other what, nine, ten, eleven by my count. At thirty-five."

"Got to dicker, eh?" Pinto asked, grinning. "Well, forty's fair, and I'll hold to it."

"Told you he was a horse thief, didn't I, boys?" Toney asked, turning to the youngsters only now stepping past their mother's shadow. "But Pinto does know his horses."

"We need 'em, too, Pa," the oldest, a straw-haired boy of ten, pointed out. "Paid more, too."

"Hush!" a flustered Bob Toney shouted.

"He's right, Pinto," Ophelia agreed. "He's got the money. Leave the stableboys to tend your animals and come along inside. I've got a pot of coffee on the stove, and biscuits in the warmer. I can tell you haven't eaten anything. Have you?"

"No, ma'am," Pinto confessed.

"Then come on along," she insisted. "Bobby, Jonathan, you help Mr. Lowery inside. Maybe later he'll have a tale or two to share about when he and your father fought for General Lee in Virginia."

The older boy, Bobby, and his brother Jonathan raced out, grabbed a Lowery arm, and escorted Pinto into the kitchen. In no time he was chewing biscuits and sharing stories.

"You been on the trail to Kansas, too, haven't you?" Bobby asked a bit later.

"Be on de trail yerself 'fore long, I'd guess," Pinto replied.

"No, he's got some growing ahead of him," Toney argued. "Ain't the same trail as when we went up there in '71. More'n Indians to worry a cowboy now."

"What?" Pinto asked.

"Oh, falling prices. Expenses. Finding good horses. If you hadn't come along, I'd have had to mount three or four men on swaybacks. Used to be you just sent out word you were putting a herd together, and you had all the men and horses you could shake a stick at. And once you finished the trail, there was money for a fine bonus and a whale of a celebration. Nowadays, who knows?"

"That bad?"

"Oh, it's not the half of it," Toney said, frowning. "Just one hard time following another. Makes a man yearn for the old, simple times like we had at Sharpsburg. Might be a hundred thousand Yanks to fight, but at least you knew who the enemy was. And where. I got to trust Jake with the range crew, you know. Don't dare leave Ophelia and the youngsters here alone, not with Comanches and renegade whites about. Just a month ago a neighbor boy got himself killed by Big Nose Joe Hannigan."

"Yeah?"

"Heard of him? The worst sort, those Hannigans. Hit the telegraph office in Weatherford. Then, leaving town, they shot little Doyle Harper for sport."

"They anywhere near?" Pinto asked nervously.

"No, but I'd wager they'll be through here once the trail herds turn north. Many a ranch'll be easy pickings then."

"Includin' dis one?" Pinto asked.

"No, I'll be staying this year, and I hired myself a fellow named Walsh. Used to be a deputy up in Jacksboro."

"Met him once," Pinto said sourly. "Bit too free with his gun for my likin'."

"Well, it'll be a comfort having a spare man who knows how to handle himself in a fight."

"Jake'll need help goin' north, though," Pinto said as he lifted his coffee cup off the table. "And me, I'll be needin' some work. What would you say to signin' me on?"

"Pinto, you've got the quickest rope hand I ever saw, but you don't have the patience for trailing cattle. Forgotten what dust tastes like? I couldn't pay you spit, either."

"Whatever it'd be would be fair."

"Lots of hands wander the range, old friend, and there are pitiful few herds heading north. I'm about to put four hundred forty dollars in your pocket. Get drunk! Have a time or two. Leave the trail to the youngsters."

"I that old?" Pinto howled. "Still got de sass to run down range ponies. And you know well and true how I am in a fight."

"Yeah, I do," Toney admitted. "But I've hired a full outfit, Pinto.

Young, sure, but so's Jake. I send you along, he'll think I don't trust him. And I'd have to leave a boy home whose ma needs the wages to feed her kids."

Pinto stared at the sorrowful face of his old friend.

"Don't worry yerself over it," Pinto said. "I got horses lef' to take into market. You need any more?"

"Got my string now," Toney said, "but if . . ."

"Was only askin'," Pinto insisted. "I can do some business in Weatherford."

"Weatherford's a poor town for horse buyers," Toney asserted. "But up north a bit you'll run across Defiance. There's the place. There are two or three ranches out that way looking for drovers, too, as I hear it. Double R, run by a fair fellow name of Richardson, is the biggest. Best, too.

"Might look him up."

"And after, if you need a place to winter, don't forget you've got friends in Parker County," Ophelia Toney declared.

"We'd make room for you ready enough," Bobby promised.

"Then you could tell us how you trapped that black stallion," Jonathan added.

"Got time for that right now," Pinto said, forcing a grin onto his face.

As it turned out, he passed the whole day with the Toney boys, sharing tales both true and imagined. The admiring glow in those boys' eyes warmed a man, even a weary mustanger accustomed to the whining wind and howling coyotes.

"Was a fine visit we had," Pinto declared as dusk settled over the Lazy T. "'Preciate you all makin' me feel so at home. Time I got back do my horses, though."

"Nonsense," Ophelia argued. "You can't mean to leave now! The boys have filled a mattress for you, and they'll howl like mad coyotes if we let you go."

"I admit it's temptin', ma'am, but I lef' enough places to know de trade. Don't get easier put off. Now's as good a time as another to ride."

"Won't you reconsider, Pinto?" Toney asked.

"You got yer ranch, Bob," Pinto said, mustering a grin. "Me, I only know de Llano. And I worry after my ponies."

With that said, he waved farewell and started for the corral. The big black sensed his approach and stirred anxiously. In short order Pinto had the restless stallion saddled. Only then did the horse stamp and storm.

"Miss dem mares, do you?" Pinto whispered. "Well, dey los' to you now, old fellow. Might's well know it."

The horse settled down, and Pinto climbed atop the saddle. Then the two of them, horse and rider, set off onto the Llano Estacado. Soon they were splashing across the Brazos and swinging west toward the walled-up canyon and the pony herd.

Chapter 5

That night Pinto made his camp beside the river in a hollow formed by a curling creek. It was a good spot, for scrub cedars and swaying willows clung to the river's banks, hiding the encampment from the eyes of any wandering Comanche or renegade cow thief. Even so, Pinto built no fire. There was a chill to the spring air, and he would have welcomed the warmth of burning embers. Even a hint of flame showed out against the black emptiness of the plain, however, and Pinto desired no unwelcome visitors—not with money enough in his boot to tempt half the state!

With the wind howling eerily through the treetops, and the black stallion pawing the ground restlessly, Pinto found himself remembering the laughter of the Toney youngsters. Laughter was a balm for a lonely man. A tonic for his troubles. But when it came time to leave, the haunting memory of high spirits could plague a man to his grave.

"You feel it too, don't you, boy?" Pinto called to the horse. "Miss bein' 'round yer own kind. Well, cain't much blame you. I miss bein' 'round mine sometimes."

All in all, though, Pinto supposed horses to be a higher caliber of creature than people. Perhaps the stallion had better cause to complain.

He passed a fitful night in the hollow. Three times the stirring of the stallion woke him. And twice the spectral face of Jamie Haskell brought Pinto shivering and shuddering to life.

"Can't you leave me be, Jamie?" Pinto howled. "I was always a true friend to you. Can't you stay dead even one night?"

Dawn found him sitting in a cold sweat and staring at the rising sun. His eyes were wild with torment, and he welcomed the resumption of his journey. Riding along the Brazos, heading back to the waiting horses gave Pinto Lowery purpose. And the work would free his mind from the iron grip of old ghosts.

Perhaps that was why he saddled the white-faced mustang and climbed atop without bothering to even chew a scrap of jerked beef. The big stallion was equally anxious to return to the penned-up ponies, and the horse sped across the broken country as if he'd become winged Pegasus.

More than once Pinto swept past startled farmboys, busy breaking ground or thinning plants. Those straw-hatted youngsters gazed up in wonder or howled encouragement at the scraggly looking stranger riding that devil of a black horse.

"What's the hurry, mister?" one called.

"You seen Indians?" another cried.

They were too young to understand it was ghosts that drove a man to such exertions. Or maybe they were smart enough to know a spectre wasn't about to be put off by such tactics.

Pinto returned to the fenced-off canyon an hour short of dusk. There'd been a rain, and the ravine was awash with runoff.

"Jus' as well," Pinto remarked as he rolled off the side of his horse and left the stallion to satisfy his thirst. "Means de ponies got plenty to drink."

He knelt beside the bubbling stream and splashed water onto his sweat-streaked face. The lines under his eyes and those etched in his forehead warned exhaustion approached. Pinto shrugged, then stripped the saddle, knapsack, and blanket from the weary stallion. It took but a moment to lead the horse to the gate and send him rushing eagerly back to his harem.

A less practical man, watching the mustangs cavorting in the natural corral, would certainly have set the whole batch loose on the Llano. The scene touched Pinto's heart. But he'd grown used to the big stallion, and the time for running free across the unbounded plain was nearly gone. Those buffalo bones proved that. No, the longhorn had come to displace both the buffalo and the range pony.

"And farmers've come to take ole Pinto's place," he lamented.

Pinto shook off the notion and set off for the river. He shed his dusty clothes and splashed into the shallows. For close to a whole hour he alternately splashed around midstream and soaked in the shallows. Finally he gave his clothes a similar scrub before snaring a pair of fat catfish for supper. As he built up a brisk fire and huddled beside it, naked save for a rough wool blanket draped around his shoulders, he couldn't help recalling similar spring eves passed with Jamie Haskell on old Abner Polland's place outside of Marshall.

"Now that's a chicken-brained notion if ever I heard one!" Jamie had howled the time Pinto suggested hiring themselves out to a pair of Choctaw traders. "Them Indians'll get a year's work out of you and pay you with some ole nag no right-minded Texan would climb onto."

"Be my own horse, though," Pinto had argued. "And I never knew any Choctaw to back out of a bargain."

"Still, it's addled thinkin', Pinto."

"Be an advendure."

"Naw, only hard work," Jamie grumbled. "I know horses some myself, don't I? My uncle raises good ones. These fool paints, Georgie, just ain't worth a lick o' salt. You got to get yer thinkin' straight."

So it was Pinto turned down the Choctaws. Isaac Flowers took the job and came home with the finest bay mare anyone north of Waco had seen. Isaac ran five hundred horses nowadays, or so Pinto had heard. Of course no Flowers, man or boy, signed the muster book and shouldered a rifle for the cause.

"Things'd been different if de war hadn't happened, Jamie," Pinto said, glancing at the phantom face smiling at him from the fire. "Who knows? You might've talked Sarah Ames into sittin' with you at Sunday meetin'. Or maybe . . ."

The dancing demon frowned, and Pinto reached over and grabbed a knife. As he started skinning the catfish, Jamie's face seemed to fade.

"Sure, things might've been different," Pinto said again. "But a man plays de hand he gets. You did, didn't you, Jamie? So now you're only a ghos' goin' 'round hauntin' yer ole friends. And me? I guess I'm still that chicken-brained fool!"

Perhaps it was lying beside the glowing embers of the fire that night that brought Pinto Lowery contentment. Or maybe the refreshing dip in the Brazos and the tasty fried catfish restored his old energies. Then, too, it might have been ghosts who took a rest from their eternal wanderings. Whatever the reason, Pinto awoke that next day with new vigor.

Almost at once he set about readying himself for a summer on the cattle trails. The paint he'd ridden for two years became a second packhorse. Pinto led the two pack animals, together with the big black and the dancing chestnut mare, beyond the fence so they could graze on the tender meadow grass downstream. He then began organizing the remaining sixteen animals for the journey back to Wise County. If they brought as fair a price as the first batch, Pinto Lowery would find himself downright close to prosperous, chicken-brain or not!

Pinto thought it likely. After all, three of the mares were long and sleek, the kind favored by Texans for breeding. The others would make good saddle ponies, and the two young stallions were sure to draw some cowboy's eye.

"Be a fair start toward a future," Pinto told himself. After all, a thousand dollars would buy a fair stretch of country. It had long been a distant dream. But just then Pinto could only think of the trail to Wichita. He remembered the singing . . . missed the pranks and the company. And the idea of another week alone with only ghosts for company vexed him considerably.

"So, it's back down de Brazos, eh?" Pinto asked.

He passed two more days readying himself and the stock for the journey, though. Those last horses were far more restless than the first batch, and Pinto draped a rope around each animal's neck and tied the whole batch to a long line he trailed behind the black. Of course, a sudden stampede would likely pull Pinto, saddle and all, across half of Texas, but so long as the horses stayed calm, they would trail well enough.

When Pinto finally did set off, he wasted little time whittling down his inventory. There were twenty or thirty ranches between that ravine-scarred valley and the little town of Defiance, and Pinto had marked each one in his mind on the homebound leg of his earlier ride. Now he visited those ranches, each in turn.

"That mare with the splash o' brown on her rump's a likely enough breeder," the first rancher observed. "But forty dollars? I ain't seen that much foldin' money in a month o' Sundays!"

At the next place a bowlegged rancher named Jonas Brayville picked out five of the more ordinary ponies.

"I know you'll get yer price on dem others," Brayville told Pinto. "But these here's sound enough, and you might take thirty-five for 'em if I was to buy the five."

"The price's forty," Pinto said, frowning. "You wouldn't talk down a hones' man from a fair price, would you?"

"I'd talk my own grandma out o' her hat if I needed it to keep my ranch goin'," Brayville insisted. "Been some lean times, you know. Comanches come through here and run off my saddle horses. Kilt my second boy. Only fourteen, he was. No bigger'n a peapod."

"Well, I know 'bout hard luck," Pinto said, relenting. "You take de five at thirty-five."

"Bless you fer a good man," Brayville responded. He went inside his house for a bit. He returned with a stack of well-worn greenbacks and three gold pieces. His wife brought a flour sack full of food and a fresh-baked pie. A shaggy-haired boy of sixteen helped his father lead the mustangs to a waiting corral while two barefooted girls herded four younger Brayvilles out of harm's way.

"We'd have you take this food for yer kindness," Brayville said when he accepted Pinto's bill of sale. "Maybe we'll pass you on the way north. You did say you thought to join a drive."

"Hopin' to," Pinto said, tying the flour sack behind his saddle. "They say they's hirin' at de Double R, up Wise County way. 'Course I still got horses to sell firs'."

"I wouldn't expect that to trouble you long," Brayville declared. "Man's hard put to find a mustang as lively as these here."

Pinto nodded his thanks for the food and the praise. Then he set off eastward again.

Gradually the string of horses melted away. A livery in Fincherville took two. One of the better mares was snatched up by a farmer north of Weatherford, and his brother-in-law rode down to Pinto's camp on the Brazos to buy another.

"Those two are of a kind," the fellow pointed out. "Can't have Henry gettin' the upper hand on me."

So it was that by the time Pinto rode into Defiance, he had only seven range ponies left. He still had his packhorses, the white-faced black, and the little chestnut, but then he had no yen to sell those. Once he had a good look at Defiance, he decided the prospects for selling anything were none too good.

Defiance, Texas, wasn't much more of a town than Hill's Junction. In fact there was only a motley collection of picket houses clustered around a brick-fronted bank, a plank-walled rooming house, and two saloons. Pinto saw one solitary figure trudging along the single dusty street, and that was a sawed-off boy whose tattered trousers hung down on his slim hips so low they threatened any second to commit an indecency. Anyone who cared to might count the child's ribs, for the leathery skin of his chest was stretched so tight that each bone seemed to protrude like a regular ridge.

"Come fer the auction, mister?" the boy called out.

"Came to sell some horses," Pinto answered.

"Buyers done gone," the boy explained. "I could have me a look 'round the drinkin' spots and see if any's stuck, though. If a man paid me two bits fer it."

"Have a look," Pinto said, tossing the youngster a quarter. The urchin snatched the coin out of the air with an unexpected dexterity and then rushed toward the nearest saloon. Amid a howl of laughter, the youngster tumbled back out the door.

"I tole you, Johnny Cole, I don't abide scarecrows in my parlor!" a tall red-haired woman announced.

"Was lookin' fer him," young Johnny said, pointing to Pinto, who nodded.

"Well, I'll excuse him for bein' a stranger," the woman said, smiling at Pinto. "You know better."

Thereupon the boy turned and made a dash toward the second saloon. He made no immediate exit from that one, and Pinto led his horses over to where he could tie them off to a hitching rail. He just finished securing the last of the animals when Johnny Cole emerged from the dingy door of the saloon, tugging the arm of a respectable-looking rancher.

"Boy, I've seen all the horses I ever care to gaze upon!" the man complained. "Now leave me to enjoy an honest game of cards in peace."

"Ain't honest if you play with Kansas Jack," the boy argued. "And there's a fellow here with horses he wants to sell."

"Were a dozen of 'em this morn," the man barked. "I've seen 'em. Now git!"

Only then did the man happen to glance around and spy Pinto. For a moment the rancher paused.

"You weren't at the auction, were you?" he called to Pinto.

"Didn't know 'bout it," Pinto explained. "Jus' come off de Llano."

"Well, you couldn't've planned it better so far's I'm concerned," the rancher declared as he trotted closer and began looking over the horses. "That chestnut mare's a dandy."

"Ain't that one fer sale," Pinto replied. "It's de seven there on de end."

"I see. Well, the roan's a stumblefoot, I'd guess, and that mare with the white tail's a hair young. Far stallion, too. I'll take the other four if the price is right."

"Forty for de three mares. Fifty for de stallion. He's a runner."

"I won't even dicker," the man said, nodding. "It's close to what I'd ask myself. I'm out a dollar or two gettin' 'em shod, but they look used to a hard life. That'll get up the trail to Kansas."

"Should," Pinto agreed. "You headin' out soon?"

"Once my neighbor gets his herd formed. We travel paired these days. Renegades and all, you know."

"Sure," Pinto said, scrawling his name across a bill of sale while the rancher counted out two hundred and ten dollars.

"Lowery, eh?" the man said as they made the exchange. "You sold a pony or two to Bob Toney."

"Sure did," Pinto admitted. "Bob and me soldiered some."

"Well, I was with the Second Texas till they took us prisoner at Vicksburg. J. B. Dotham's the name."

"George Lowery," Pinto said, grinning. "'Course mos' call me Pinto. For my way with mustangs."

"Name's apt enough, Pinto. Why don't you come along into the Lucky Seven here with me and cool off. You look to've had a fair ride. Don't play cards, do you?"

"Not with nobody calls himself Kansas Jack," Pinto said, flashing a smile at little Johnny Cole. "Would like to ged thad boy somethin' do eat, though."

"Ramon, is it too late to buy a platter of tamales?" Dotham asked a pleasant-looking young Mexican.

"No, I fix 'em," Ramon answered. "Johnny Cole, you come on to the kitchen. Mama will feed you."

"Thanks," Pinto said, tossing Ramon a silver dollar. Ramon waved to the boy, and the two of them trotted around the bar and found the kitchen. Pinto, meanwhile, sat at a table alongside J. B.

Dotham. The rancher poured out two glasses of smoky-looking liquid and passed one to Pinto.

"It passes for whiskey," Dotham explained. "Does settle the dust."

"I thank you, sir," Pinto replied as he raised his glass and drank to the health of his new acquaintance.

"It's me's been done the service," Dotham countered. "I'll at least have four men well-mounted on the trail."

Before Pinto could reply, a young cowboy rose from the gaming table and slammed a pistol barrel across the forehead of the dandy to his right.

"Won't Kansas Jack cheat another cowboy this day!" the young drover announced as he held up a handful of banknotes.

Two other players carried the Kansan over to a bench and set him there to recover. The game then resumed.

"Bunch o' fools," Dotham grumbled. "Cowboys! Children! Drink too much and talk too much and ain't worth half the wages I pay 'em. Still, they get my cows to the railhead."

"Yeah, and if dey lissen some, dey live to learn better," Pinto declared. The two went on talking another hour. Pinto tried to bring the conversation around to the upcoming trail drive, but Dotham had his mind on horses and wouldn't be distracted.

That was when Ramon swept Johnny Cole out of the kitchen. The ragged youngster hopped out past the bar and fell against the gaming table, upsetting a near-empty whiskey bottle and bringing the cowboys to their feet.

"Fool boy," the nearest one shouted, lifting young Cole off the ground by the chin and flinging him hard against the wall. The little boy bounded off the hard oak planks and fell in a whimpering heap. As if that wasn't enough, the cowboy drove the toe of his boot into the small of the youngster's back.

"That's about enough o' that!" Pinto exclaimed as he rose to his feet and slid over to block the next kick.

"I don't see this's any o' yer business, pop!" the cowboy said, backing a step and throwing open his jacket. A polished leather holster holding a Colt revolver hugged his right hip.

"I didn't come here do shoot anybody," Pinto said as he helped a shaken Johnny Cole off the floor. "Boy, bes' run along and find a place to hide a time."

"Yessir," Johnny said, darting out the door.

"Now, it's settled, eh?" Pinto asked.

"Not by half," the cowboy answered. "You done butted into my business. You got to pay for that."

"How much?" Pinto asked, souring. "Fifty cends cover it?"

That made the red-faced cowboy madder. He tapped fingers on his hip and stared coldly at Pinto's face.

"You ever shot anybody, Danny?" Dotham suddenly asked.

"About to," the cowboy answered.

"Well this fellow's kilt a dozen Yankees in his time up in Virginia. Look to that left hand there. See where the bullet's sawed a finger down to size. Now look him in the eye. No sweat on his forehead. He'll shoot back, boy."

"I'm fast, Mr. Dotham."

"He'll kill you just the same," Dotham argued. "And won't be happy doin' it, either, I'm guessin'. Son, there's those here who'd judge you not the wronged man here. That boy was clumsy, but he's just a snip of a child and didn't merit yer boot. You'll find later on dyin' ought to follow a better grievance. Drink a little less and apologize a trifle more. That'd be my advice. I can't afford to lose a man before even settin' out for Kansas."

"But he—"

"Get yerself back to the ranch, Danny Elton, before I lose *my* temper. Hear?"

"Yes, sir," the cowboy reluctantly agreed.

"You others, too," the rancher commanded, and the remaining drovers stumbled toward the door.

"You did that jus' fine," Pinto observed.

"Ain't bad boys," Dotham said by way of apology. "Just young. All I got, though."

"Shorthanded?" Pinto asked.

"Not as you'd know it. Twenty-eight men, and that's just my half of the outfit."

"I thought maybe you might need another man."

"You? I could, Lowery, but I signed on a full crew," Dotham explained. "I wouldn't be able to pay you, and I never hire a job done I can't pay for. Breeds ill feelings."

"Sure," Pinto said, dropping his gaze.

"Still, there's my partner. And neighbor. Ryan Richardson. He runs the Double R. Might buy them other horses, too. Just head north from town. Toward Decatur. Three miles up and on yer right. Can't miss it. House is a big one with a gabled roof."

"Might ride out and have a talk with him."

"Tell him I suggested it. And that you know Bob Toney."

"Sure," Pinto said, turning toward the door. "Thanks fer de conversation, Mr. Dotham. Good luck to you, too."

"Might be I'll need it," Dotham muttered. "Good luck to you as well."

"Might need some my own self," Pinto answered as he stepped out the door. Might indeed!

Chapter 6

The Double R Ranch wasn't at all what Pinto had expected. On the short ride out from Defiance he'd seen only the same windswept plain and spotted hills that spread north of Fort Worth toward the Red River. But now, east of the dusty market road, a tall gabled house rose from a grove of peach trees. It was as if Pinto Lowery had suddenly been swept through time and space to one of the Virginia manor houses encountered during his soldier days.

"It's a place to remember," Pinto remarked. And he judged Ryan Richardson to be that sort of man, too. Not many who had lived through the dark days of the war and the hard times that followed had kept dreams kindled. Pinto Lowery hadn't. This Richardson, though, was even now adding rooms off the west side of his house. Moreover, the walls were built of flat gray stone. Yes, here was a place to last.

Pinto couldn't help staring at the wide veranda and the tall, symmetrical windows that flanked two heavy wooden front doors. Even when he dismounted, his eyes remained on the grand house. So it was that when a gangly boy of fifteen or so suddenly called out, Pinto responded with a start.

"Talkin' at me?" Pinto cried.

"Nobody else's come ridin' up to my house with half a dozen horses," the sandy-haired youngster barked. "Got business here?"

"Thought to have," Pinto answered, giving the big black a stroke across his white nose and nodding at the other animals. "Name's Lowery. I raise horses."

"These look to've raised 'emselves," the boy pointed out. "Range ponies. 'Cept for that chestnut there. She's no accident."

"No, sir," Pinto agreed. "Half a year's labor paid for her. But that's not what brung me here. I come through Defiance town and sold some animals to a fellow name o' Dotham. Plans to take the trail north to Kansas, as he tells it. Said de Double R's goin' with him, and I might sell dese three saddle ponies to a fellow name o' Richardson."

"That'd be my pa," the boy answered. He paused a moment to study Pinto's face. Then he glanced over the horses. "He ain't here just now," the boy finally explained.

"Yeah?" Pinto asked.

"Out with the range crew. I guess I could take you to him. In a bit."

"You'd be de only man about, wouldn't you?" Pinto asked, reading the wariness in the fifteen-year-old's eyes. "You jus' point de way. I got a nose fer findin' people."

"I'd have to know a man better to send him Pa's way," the boy said.

Pinto glanced around the buildings. A pair of smaller boys had started over from a chicken coop. A winsome girl in her late teens now appeared in the doorway.

"Who's that come visitin', Jared?" she called.

"Mustanger named Lowery," Jared answered. "I was thinkin' to take him to see Pa."

"Not 'fore supper, you won't," she answered. "Your friend there looks like he could stand a good feedin', too."

"Could be you'd feel easier if I was on my way," Pinto said, recognizing the concern etched in Jared Richardson's brow.

"No, if Mr. Dotham sent you along, I don't figure you to do us harm," Jared responded. "You might leave that pistol off your hip, though. Elsewise Jim and Job'll talk off your ear on it."

"Sure," Pinto agreed. "Got a Parker County friend with boys like to jabber."

"Who'd that be?" Jared asked as he helped Pinto secure the horses.

"Bob Toney. Lazy T."

"I've rid some miles with him," Jared declared, grinning. "He and his boys both. Should've said that right off. Lowery, huh? I recall him speakin' of you. Judged you to have the devil's own way with horses, though you could be mule-stubborn and chicken-brained besides."

"Guess he has spoke o' me," Pinto said, laughing. "That's ole Bob. You ask him sometime who drug him off de field at Spotsylvania Court House? Was dis chicken-brained fool here!"

Jared echoed Pinto's cackle. The youngster went on to introduce his brothers Jim and Job before turning to the pleasant-faced young woman in the doorway.

"Now this's Arabella," Jared explained. "Our sister. She sort o' runs the house, what with Ma bein' dead."

"Sort o'?" ten-year-old Job asked. Jim, who was a hair younger, couldn't resist a chance to laugh.

"I heard o' kings easier o' manner," Jared whispered. "Don't you get the wrong side o' Arabella. Not if you figure to see tomorrow."

"Works us near to death," Job added.

"Work?" Arabella exclaimed. "What would you useless batch o' fool boys know o' work! Now get washed and come to supper. It's sure grown cold."

"More likely burnt black," little Job said, hopping out of his sister's reach. Jim chuckled again, and Arabella gave him a solid swat. She then marched down a long hall to the kitchen. Pinto followed Jared in that same direction while the younger Richardsons set off to find a wash basin.

Supper with the Richardson youngsters took Pinto back to his own younger years. His sisters had been a considerable vexation, and though he hadn't had brothers to provide like torment, there'd been cousins aplenty to stand in their place.

"You'll find no escape from troubles in the army, Georgie," his mother had warned when he joined the Marshall Guards. But being young, Pinto hadn't believed that. There never was a hint of smarts an older person could pass along to a young one. No, things had to be learned all over again . . . and again . . . and again.

After stuffing himself with three helpings of Arabella Richardson's meat loaf, four potatoes, and a fair assortment of greens, Pinto finally accompanied Jared back outside.

"The crew's sure to be havin' its supper, too," the boy announced. "Pa'll be tired, but I don't figure he'll be past hagglin' over horses. He's a fair hand at tradin', folks say."

"Well, that ought to make fer a well-passed evenin'," Pinto declared as he collected his horses. As he climbed atop the big black, Jared ran his hand along the flank of the chestnut mare.

"Don't suppose I might have a ride on her, do you?" Jared asked. "Just the three miles or so to the range camp."

"Get her saddled," Pinto answered. "But don't hurry her along. She's not used to carryin' anybody."

"I'll be easy on her," the boy promised. "You see I don't wear spurs. Don't even dig my toes in like some I know. Truth is I never needed to. Horses sort o' take to me."

"That's 'cause you smell like one," Job hollered from a nearby corral. "Can we come along, Jared?" Jim said, glancing up hopefully.

"Be late comin' home," Jared told them. "We'll have ourselves a ride tomorrow."

The smaller boys nodded soberly, then dashed off to find some other mischief. Jared soon had the mare saddled. Then he climbed atop the spry chestnut and led the way northward. Pinto followed.

It took but a quarter hour, even riding slow, to reach the range camp. Along the way Pinto eyed the two thousand grazing longhorns that would make up the Double R trail herd. Some of the animals bore other brands, Pinto noted. Richardson was probably taking on other than J. B. Dotham's steers.

That was, indeed, the case.

"Pa's got close to every man in Wise County out here," Jared explained as they rode. "Times's been tough lately, and we all got our hopes pinned on sellin' these steers for a high profit."

"You got de jump on de south Texas crews," Pinto said. "Bet you'll get yer price."

"Trailin' cattle's a regular adventure, I hear."

"Can be," Pinto admitted. "I recall a high time or two. More'n one nightmare, though. Near got drowned once and trampled twice."

"Done it, have you?"

"Twice."

"How come you ain't signed on with somebody this year?" Jared asked.

"Nobody's been fool enough to take me on," Pinto said, laughing. "Truth is, I hoped yer pa'd have a place."

"Won't even take me," Jared grumbled. "But it might be different with a full-grown man."

"You look man aplenty to me," Pinto replied. "Likely yer pa wants somebody to watch over yer brothers and sister."

"He says that," Jared muttered. "But he's taken along others littler with mas and brothers barely past diapers."

Pinto tried to think of something to say to the boy, but after all, words weren't much of a tonic for hurt insides. Besides, the camp appeared on a nearby hill. Jared nudged the chestnut mare into a trot, and the two of them ushered the other horses between them.

"Son, what's brought you out here?" asked a tall, broad-shouldered man wearing a tan stiff-brimmed hat.

"Pa, I brought Mr. Lowery along," Jared explained. "You remember Bob Toney talkin' about him. He's got three horses to sell off. Thought you could use 'em maybe."

"Thought right," the rancher responded. "Lowery, I'm Ryan

Richardson. Slide along down and let's dicker. These three, huh? What of the chestnut Jared's ridin'?"

"She's special," the boy answered as he dismounted. "Mr. Lowery's also lookin' to sign on with a trail crew."

"Well, Mr. Lowery and I'll do business on the first count anyway," Richardson announced.

"Ain't no mister to me," Pinto said as he climbed down from the big black. "Call me Pinto."

"I'm Ryan," Richardson said, accepting Pinto's proffered hand. "These three look sound. I pay twenty-five for saddle ponies, but I judge you'll want more."

"Forty's fair," Pinto answered. "If you want to dicker, best call it fifty. Make you feel you got me down some when I sell 'em fer forty."

"Forty's fair," Richardson agreed. "I'll count out the cash."

While Richardson walked off a moment, Jared stepped over and stared longingly at the chestnut.

"If you'd sell her, Pinto, I'd see she got treated easy," the boy whispered. "I got seventy dollars saved up. Come by honest, too. Ask Pa. Mostly from workin' deerhides or helpin' neighbors get in their corn."

"I figured to breed her," Pinto explained.

"Know that," the boy confessed. "But I'd see you got a colt by and by. Seventy dollars ain't much of a price, I merit, but it's what I got in my boot."

Pinto turned from the boy to the horse. The two were a pair. There was no denying it. Sometimes a horse ought to go to a man who had wildfire in his heart. Jared sat down and pulled off his boot. He held out a fistful of crumpled notes, and Pinto grinned.

"Done," the mustanger agreed, taking the money and gripping the youngster's hand.

"Hear that?" Jared asked, hugging the chestnut's neck. "You're mine, girl."

"What?" Richardson asked as he rejoined them. "You bought that mare, son? You must be a better haggler than me."

"Oh, I wouldn't wager that," Jared replied. "It's just I watched him with those horses. He knew I wanted her bad."

"You'd never make a proper rancher," Richardson said as he paid Pinto for the mustangs. "No love o' hagglin' and too much heart. Still, I thank you for makin' a youngster happy."

"You could return de favor," Pinto said, stuffing the money into his pocket and scrawling his name on two bills of sale. "I had in my mind headin' north dis summer."

"I got a full crew," Richardson said, sighing. "Look out there. Two thousand head. A third's from neighbors, and they'll slow us down fattenin' up. Look around at my outfit now. Lord, I got near every boychild with chin whiskers for fifty miles around. And a few without."

"Some o' those boys won't make it pas' de Nations," Pinto said sadly. "I know. I been dere. Look yonder at that one. Cain't even get his toes in his stirrups!"

"I made promises to my neighbors," Richardson explained. "Joe Bill Trask there's as close to a man's that family's got. Wages he earns'll keep hunger from his door. People hereabouts have had it hard. Money's needed to pay taxes and buy seed. Their kids want shoes and such. Can't take a stranger and leave a friend to suffer."

"Unnerstand that," Pinto muttered. "But a man needs a purpose to put himself too."

"Sure, he does," Richardson agreed. "Tell you what. I've signed on Tully Oakes and his boy Truett. They've got a nice enough place, and they put in a good crop of corn. Could be they'd favor havin' a man around to keep watch over that corn."

"Ain't a farmer."

"Likely Tully could do with a man to watch Elsie and the little ones, too," Richardson added.

"That makes a difference, do it?"

"Let me sketch you a map that'll get you to the Oakes place," Richardson offered. "You tell Tully I sent you over."

"Pa, I'll take him," Jared offered. "Be good to visit a hair with Tru."

"Don't you jaw the night away, son. I've got words to share with you tomorrow. We'll be headin' north directly. I have things to tell you and Arabella."

"Sure," Jared agreed.

"Be best not to send you ridin' out that way by twilight," Richardson said, turning back to Pinto. "But tomorrow the Oakes men'll be busy. Time to make a bargain's tonight. Set you a fair price, too, Pinto. In writin'. Tully's never been one to recall his agreements."

"I'll write it up myself," Jared promised. "By way o' returnin' a favor."

"Get along with you now," Richardson ordered his son. "I've got a final word for Pinto."

"Sure, Pa," Jared agreed as he turned toward the horses.

"Don't need to say it," Pinto whispered. "It's on yer face and in yer eyes. I'll give a look after 'em."

"It'd be appreciated," Richardson said, shaking Pinto's hand in a firm farewell grip. "See you get everything written down. Only way to deal with Tully Oakes."

"Sure," Pinto said, releasing Richardson's hand and heading back to where the big black stood restlessly pawing the ground. Then, with the packhorse trailing along behind, Pinto Lowery followed Jared Richardson out of the cattle camp.

Chapter 7

"Pa's done you no favors, sendin' you out to see Tully Oakes," Jared declared as they rode. "I never knew another man half as contrary as ole Tully. Truett, he's as good a friend as you'd want, and Miz Oakes's just fine, too. Ole Tully's one to watch, though. He's backslid on so many promises to Tru, well, it's hard to see why the either of 'em bothers comin' to terms. Tully'll only break 'em. Last summer Pa advanced Tully money against what the steers would bring at market. Never saw a dime of it again. Ben Moorehead put a roof on the Oakes barn, but did he get paid? Not as I heard."

"Knowin' yer pa to feel such, I wonder he steered me here," Pinto said as they approached a small picket cabin standing beside a clapboard barn. "Or why he'd take dis Oakes to Kansas with him."

"That's on account of Elsie Oakes bein' kin. Ma's cousin. As to takin' Tully, I'd guess Pa figures to get some o' his money back for the trouble last summer. He thought to leave 'em to get their own steers north, but then Elsie, Tru, and the little ones'd only starve. You ask me, it'd be better all 'round to leave Tully and take little Ben. He's nought but twelve, but I wager he'd be more use."

"Have to be a mighty hard twelve to make it to Wichita," Pinto said, frowning. "Sometimes hardship gives a man backbone, too. Maybe dis Dully Oakes jus' needs a chance."

"Maybe," Jared said. He wasn't half convinced.

Shortly Pinto was to have a chance to judge matters for himself, though. A shaggy-haired boy, lean and hard for fourteen, stepped out from the house and called a friendly hello.

"What's got you out here with dark on its way, Jared?" the boy asked as he trotted over. "And where'd you come by that mare? She's too fine for you by half."

"Meet Pinto Lowery, Tru," Jared replied. "He's a horse chaser from out west a bit. Bought this mare off him."

"I could use a horse, Jared, but you know we got no cash to spare. Sorry, mister, but you won't find much market here."

"Sold my string," Pinto explained. "Mr. Richardson bought de las' three off me."

"So what brings you to our place?" Truett asked anxiously.

"Mr. Richardson advised it," Pinto explained. "Said yer pa might could use a hand do watch over his acreage while he was off to Kansas."

"Tru's goin', too," Jared added. "Nobody full-growed to look after things."

"Ben and Brax can do what chores need doin'," a gruff voice announced from behind. Pinto turned in time to see a big, broad-backed giant of a man march out from the barn. With a bearlike paw Tully Oakes pushed back tangles of oily black hair from his forehead.

"They won't be much help if Comanches happen by," Jared announced. "Nor for seein' the corn gets water if we have another dry June. Pa figured somebody ought to think about Elsie."

"Meanin' I don't?" Tully stormed.

"That'd be for Pa to answer," Jared answered coldly. "Anyhow, Pinto's here. You hire him or not as you like. I'm headin' home. Pa expects you at his camp early tomorrow. Ain't altogether pleased you didn't help with the brandin'."

"Was busy here," Tully insisted. "Headin' out tomorrow?"

"With or without you," Jared said as he turned the chestnut mare southward. "Good luck to you, Pinto. Might be you'll need it. And don't forget what I said."

Pinto waved young Richardson farewell. Then the weary mustanger rolled off his horse and eyed Tully Oakes.

"Don't know I'd bother gettin' down," Tully barked. "You ain't stayin'."

"Den I'll get back on top and make some miles," Pinto said, shrugging his shoulders.

"Hold on, Pa," Truett objected. "He's come this far. Cousin Ryan and Jared never would've sent him without a reason. We'll have money once we sell off our beeves, but it won't build a new house nor be much of a swap for a scorched corn crop."

"Look at him, son," Tully argued. "I seen these drifters. They hit their horse runnin' first chance that comes along, so I wouldn't figure him to help much if Comanches came raidin'."

"I never run from trouble yet," Pinto said, staring hard at the big farmer. "If you'd care to try me, roll up yer sleeves and have at it."

"Look there, Pa," Truett said, grabbing Pinto's hand and showing the old scars. "That's a bullet done that, I'd bet."

"And put the sad in the eyes, too," Elsie Oakes said, stepping out to join her husband and eldest son. Two smaller boys and a girl of eight kept to their mother's shadow.

"Many a cattle thief's been shot," Tully muttered.

"I'd judge that uncalled fer," Pinto said, squaring off.

"Was it the war, mister?" twelve-year-old Ben asked from his mother's side.

"Sharpsburg," Pinto announced. "Maryland campaign under General Bob Lee. Firs' Texas Infantry. Never collected myself any bullet holes in de back, nor'd I leave a friend on de field if I could drag him along with me. I was ready do fight den and I am now. I'll do it, too, if I've further cause."

"You won't have," Elsie insisted. "I lost my only brother at Gettysburg."

"Got myself plucked at that place, too," Pinto said, grinning. "Dem Yanks took it particular bad me crossin' de Potomac."

"Tully?" Elsie asked, a hand planted on each hip.

"I'll agree that's a high recommendation," Oakes confessed. "Tie off yer horses and let's have ourselves a talk. Either way you'll stay the night. I feel a storm comin' on, and I never sent an honest man travellin' in the rain."

Pinto nodded, then secured his horses. Tully splashed cool water on his face and motioned to the porch. Pinto took a deep breath and walked over. As he sat beside the big farmer, Oakes began discussing terms.

"I'm not a rich man, you know," Tully began. "Truth is, I rely on sellin' my steers at a generous profit to put by enough cash to get through winter. I never paid a man to guard the farm before."

No, Pinto thought. *And you won't pay me 'less I get somethin' in writin'*.

"Had in mind five dollars a week and found," Tully suggested. "After all, you won't have much to do."

"I wouldn't chop wood fer five dollars a week," Pinto remarked. "A good hand makes fifteen. Seein' you face hard times, I'll dake ten. But takin' short wages, I'll be passin' some time ridin' 'round, runnin' in a range pony or so."

"I'd be payin' you to watch my family."

"Wouldn't be so far off as not to smell trouble," Pinto assured the farmer.

"We'll be gone a month."

"Six weeks more likely."

"I ain't got sixty dollars foldin' money do leave Elsie, much less to pay you. We'll settle up when I get home."

"Dat's a long time to wait," Pinto pointed out.

"You can trust me, Lowery!"

"A lot can happen on a cattle trail," Pinto declared. "Bes' we put it in writin'."

"Richardson's put you up to this, ain't he?"

"Spoke some on it," Pinto confessed. "Said dere'd been a disagreement o' sorts 'tween you. Better it's spelled out."

"Truett!" Tully shouted. The boy appeared, and his father ordered pen and paper. "The boy'll draw it up," Tully explained to Pinto. "I never had a talent for writin'."

"Pinto nodded his agreement, and when Truett returned, the boy set about neatly copying out the agreed-upon terms. Pinto wasn't much for reading himself, but he could understand figures well enough. And he knew the difference between five and six weeks. Errors were corrected, and after Tully Oakes made his mark, George Lowery signed the paper.

"That'll be mine to keep," Pinto announced when Tully attempted to pocket the paper. "You'll see it again when I ask fer my pay."

Tully reluctantly nodded. Then, with things settled, Tully set off walking with his wife. Truett introduced Pinto to the younger Oakes children. Afterward the three boys conducted Pinto to the barn and helped him make up a bed of straw in the loft.

"Sometimes we sleep up here, too," little Braxton explained. "It's cooler'n the house, what with the big loft door open and the wind blowin' through."

"We come up here when Pa takes to snorin' bad, too," Ben added, laughing. "Or when Jared Richardson's come fer a visit."

"Or if Tru's picked up a story from some cowboy," Brax added with a grin. "It's a good enough place."

"Better'n mos' I known," Pinto declared.

"You was in the army," Brax said. "I was named after a soldier myself. General Braxton Bragg."

"Those what served under Bragg didn't make much o' him," Pinto said sourly. "Long on punishment and short on sense, as I heard. I was with Hood mostly."

"So was our Uncle Pat," Truett explained. "The one kilt at Gettysburg. Fourth Texas."

"Was a fair portion fell at that place," Pinto told them. "Yup, more'n a few. Lucky cusses like me only picked up a scar."

Pinto showed the bent fingers of his left hand and the pale scars left by the ravishes of war. He then unbuckled his trousers and showed them the long jagged mark left by the army surgeon who had worked on his leg.

"Noticed you limpin' some," Ben whispered.

Pinto threw a nightshirt over his bony shoulders and frowned.

"Can't much tell when I'm on a horse," the ex-soldier said grimly. "But I got no speed afoot like I once did."

"Don't see where you'd need it," Truett said. "Unless it was to chase nosy boys to their beds."

"Does 'pear to be late," Pinto remarked.

Truett pointed the way to the loft ladder, and Ben began making his way to the ground. Braxton followed, and Truett brought up the rear.

"They wouldn't turn down a story after we leave," Truett said as he, too, prepared to descend the ladder. "Pa and I tell 'em tales to halt the wildness. Might be a comfort."

"Do my bes'," Pinto promised.

"Watch over Ma. She's strong-willed about things. You may have a battle if it comes to leavin' the house to escape Comanches."

"I fought Comanches lots o' times," Pinto argued. "Dey know me well enough. I don't expec' dey'll bother us. No, de varmints that plague Texas these days don't have red skins."

"Well, see they leave her be, too, if you will. She deserves better'n Pa, you know. Better'n me, too, I suppose."

"Most mamas do," Pinto said, recalling the angelic face of his own.

"I got a hard ride ahead o' me, so I'll say good night, too."

"Would seem bes'," Pinto agreed.

It was well past sunrise that next morning when the stirring of horses in the barn below roused Pinto from a sound sleep. He hadn't stayed abed past dawn since he could remember, and the realization startled him into motion. In half a shake he shed his nightshirt and scrambled into the rags that passed for clothes. By the time he was climbing down the loft ladder, Tully and Truett Oakes were already spirals of dust on the southern horizon.

"The horse man's up, Ma," Ben announced.

"Is he now?" Elsie Oakes asked, turning toward Pinto with a bemused expression. "Well, Benjamin, perhaps you'd tell the horse man that on this farm a man who wants breakfast is up with the chickens."

"De horse man knows, ma'am," Pinto said as he rubbed the mist from his eyes. "Never would've expected otherwise. Don't make a habit o' sleepin' away de mornin', you know."

"I don't know," Elsie said, frowning. "I didn't ask for anyone to stay and protect me from imagined harm, Mr. Lowery, and I won't countenance sloth. If you're here to work, then I expect no less than a full day's labor. If not, I suggest you leave immediately."

"Through?" Pinto asked.

"I said what I intended to say," she answered.

"Den you tell me what exatly you want done, and I'll set about doin' it."

"Hogs need feedin'," Ben suggested.

"That's your chore, Ben," Braxton objected.

"I suppose you could work on the corral," Elsie grumbled. "The rails aren't any too sturdy."

"You know what Pa said," Ben interrupted. "We only got ole Sugarcane in there 'sides this fellow's horses. Pa said he'd fix it by and by."

"You'll be six feet tall, by and by, Benjamin," Elsie pointed out. "I'm not sure the corral will wait that long."

"Roof needs shinglin', too," Brax said.

"It does indeed," Elsie said, grinning. "What else merits a man's attention, children?"

They provided a fair list, and Pinto leaned against a woodpile and laughed.

"Good thing a man come along," he told the Oakeses. "I'd judge you couldn't've waited much longer."

"Pa would've fixed things," Ben objected.

"Sure, I guess we all know that," Pinto said, smiling with

approval at the boy's loyalty. "But dere's jus' so much work a man can milk out o' every day."

Pinto soon had cause to wonder at the truth of that statement. That first day he reset the corral posts as they should have been placed, and by nightfall he had the rails pegged in place. Aside from a brief pause for food, he'd labored straight through.

It got no better after that. From dawn to dusk Elsie Oakes had him hammering or sawing or patching. First he cut cedars and then he made shingles. With Ben alongside to pass the slivers of cedar along, Pinto nailed one after another into place. Just when he had the end of the job in sight, the sky darkened, and lightning rattled the windows.

"Just in time!" Braxton shouted as rain began pelting the roof.

"It ain't leakin'," little Winifred cried through the doorway. "They got it fixed!"

A tremendous blast of lightning then split the heavens, and Pinto flattened himself against the roof and hung on with all his might.

"Mister, help!" Ben cried.

Pinto blinked the moisture out of his eye and searched for the boy. Ben was clinging to the chimney and shaking like a leaf. Then another flash lit the sky, and the earth shuddered. Ben's fingers slipped on the wet stone of the chimney, and he started a long slide down the sloping roof. Pinto released his own grip and made a quick stab with his right hand. He managed to grab Ben's belt and hold on, but the rain and the wind were coming in all their fury now, and there was no halting their skid.

"Grab 'hold, boy!" Pinto shouted as he felt his legs dangle off the roof.

"Lord, help us," Ben muttered as he threw his arms around the man's back and held on.

An hour earlier Pinto supposed the fall would have killed the both of them. The thundershower had converted the hard clay soil to a swimming morass of mud, though, and Pinto found himself hurled down into a wallow. Even so, it drove sharp pain up his spine. And he wasn't helped a particle by the instantaneous arrival of Ben Oakes, who had lost his grip only to land squarely atop Pinto Lowery.

For three or four minutes the two of them lay there in the mud—stunned and fighting for breath. Then Ben rolled over and sank into the mud long enough for Pinto to drink in air and recover his senses.

"Mister?" Ben whispered as he sat beside a wheezing Pinto Lowery. "Mister, you alive?"

"Yup," Pinto managed to say as he spit out a mouthful of mud. "Ben, you don't look to be much, but I'm here to tell you, you pack a fair wallop when you land on a man."

"Sorry," Ben said, digging Pinto's legs out of the bog. "I lost my grip, and I . . ."

"Nothin' to worry after," Pinto said, smiling through the mess. "Didn't break a bone, did you? Well, me neither. I'd say it come out fine all in all. We're in one piece."

"Don't speak too soon," Ben said as he pointed to Elsie Oakes, storming at them with fire in her eyes.

"Just look at you two!" she shouted. "Here, I've been worried you might be struck by lightnin', and you're floppin' in the mud like a pair o' piglets!"

"Ma, you don't understand," Ben argued.

"I understand just fine, thank you. I've near ruined my only shoes lookin' for you, Benjamin, and I find this fool mustanger's got you splashin' around in the mud."

"Ma, no," Ben said, stumbling over to prevent her from booting Pinto Lowery in the rump. "That's not how it was at all. I was slippin' down the roof. Mr. Lowery come flyin' over and grabbed me. He fell off the roof 'cause of it, and then I went and landed right atop him. Might've kilt him, Ma!"

"You fell off the roof?" Elsie cried, pulling her son to her.

"No, I had de boy all de while," Pinto objected. "If I hadn't hit so hard, I might've got us to rollin'. Weren't no danger to it."

"Not for Ben, you mean," she said, collecting her wits. "You, on the other hand . . ."

"Ma'am, dis ole fool's been Yankee shot, mustang throwed, and stomped by jus' about every hailstone and thunderclap in tarnation, and he's not dead yet. I do tell you, though, dis boy's farm hard and Texas solid. Be a man to know one o' dese days. 'Fore long, I'd wager you."

"I'm beginning to think you may be a man worth knowing yourself, Mr. Lowery," Elsie observed. "Now let's get the two of you inside the house and out of this rain."

"Barn'd be better," Pinto suggested.

"Nonsense," she argued. "I'll heat a tub and you can scrub yourself new. The both of you."

"Figure Ma to work a bath into a fall off a roof," Ben said, sighing. "Can't we just stand in the rain."

"Get along, Benjamin!" she hollered, dragging him at her side. "I'm near frozen myself, and I hesitate to wonder how Mr. Lowery feels."

"Likely sorry he's lived," Ben said, laughing. "Worse fate'n drownin' in mud. Fallin' into the hands o' womenfolk!"

Chapter 8

Actually Pinto rather welcomed the hot tub. Even as he and Ben were following Elsie inside the house, a fierce norther exploded across northern Texas, rattling windows with pellets of hail and driving temperatures lower by the minute. Rain and mud had already chilled Pinto Lowery to the bone, and now he could hardly keep his teeth from shaking his jaw off.

"Winifred, help me set another kettle to boil," Elsie called as she stumbled over beside the stove.

Pinto took one look at the inside of the small picket cabin and sighed. Lace curtains graced the windows, and there wasn't a particle of dust to be found anywhere. Now along came Pinto with his muddy boots and sodden clothes to undo all that effort.

"Ma'am, I'll muddy yer rug sure," Pinto objected.

"Well, why should you be different?" Elsie replied. "I've already done it myself, and Ben is sure to spatter his way over every inch of the place. Brax, find Mr. Lowery a blanket. He can skin himself of those wet rags in your room, can't he?"

"Sure, Ma," Braxton said, waving Pinto along as he left the comfort of a crackling fire. The ten-year-old soon guided Pinto to a small corner room holding two tiered bunks and a single hammock.

"Tru's," Brax explained when Pinto examined the hammock. "Jared Richardson's got one. Tru had Ma sew up a blanket and then hung the thing on ropes. He falls out of it nine nights out o' ten, but there's no tellin' him to pack it away. Tru's headstrong to a fault."

"Got a hair o' that bug my own self," Pinto said as he shed his muddy clothes.

"That's where the Yankees got you, huh?" Brax asked when Pinto peeled off his britches, revealing the scar on his left leg.

"Yup, that's de place," Pinto said, allowing the boy to trace the scar with a small finger. "Doc did a fine job o' stitchery, didn't he? Lots o' boys'd come up short a leg, but I went and found myself some luck that day."

Braxton nodded somberly as he rummaged through a trunk. He finally located a blanket and offered it to the shivering mustanger. With it wrapped securely around his waist, Pinto crept back toward the kitchen. A wooden tub stood in the center of the small room, and little Winifred helped her mother empty the contents of a boiling kettle into the bath.

"Ma'am, seems to me you got a chill yerself," Pinto observed as he took note of Elsie's trembling fingers. "You let me occupy myself elsewhere a few minutes and take de firs' soak."

"That's for company to take," Elsie answered.

"I'm not company," Pinto argued. "Jus' hired help. What's more I've known rough life aplenty. I'll go swing in yon hammock. Send Brax to fetch me when de time comes. And get Ben scrubbed, too."

"Mr. Lowery . . ." Elsie began.

"Now dere's another thing," Pinto interrupted. "All dis mister business's fine in its own way, but I ain't got a bone in my body to merit anybody dippin' a hat nor callin' me mister. My friends call me Pinto, dem that's not got 'emselves killed. Suits me well 'nough."

"Then it's best you call me Elsie," his weary host countered. "I'd argue with you some more, but I *am* cold, and I *will* accept your generous offer. Brax, you watch your sister. Ben, get along out of those clothes now. And keep Mister . . . Pinto . . . company."

"Yes, ma'am," Ben said, shaking his head and waving Pinto back to the small corner room. "She'll scrub my hide off with that brush, you know," the boy complained when they were safely out of his mother's earshot. "Take a year's growth off me."

"You know, Ben, dere's men pay a silver dollar in Wichita fer a scrub like what you'll get. Hold yer tongue till yer older. Man don't have a ma forever, and when she's gone, won't nobody look on you half so kind."

"You lose yer ma, Pinto?"

"Year 'fore I come back from de war," Pinto said, frowning. "And ain't a lot o' good I known since."

Ben nodded sadly as he unbuttoned his soggy shirt.

"She means well enough, I suppose," the boy added. "And I sure'd miss her if she was to not be here, like Jared's ma. But she just don't leave a man much dignity, washin' him naked like he was still a baby and not half grown."

"Sure," Pinto said, fighting the urge to grin as he stared at the spidery arms and protruding ribs of the child hurrying himself into premature manhood. It wasn't until Ben wrapped himself in a quilt and drew a mouth organ to his lips that Pinto grew cold.

"Don't you like music, Pinto?" Ben asked.

"Like it jus' dandy," Pinto replied. "Only stirred up a recollection's all."

"'Bout a harmonica player?"

"A friend," Pinto whispered. "Some'd say he was jus' a boy himself. Never saw de backbone nor de heart."

"Somethin' bad happen to him? In the war?"

Pinto nodded. In the war? Sure. In one war or another. Or was it all the same one?

Braxton came along to fetch Ben, and the brothers dragged themselves along to the kitchen. A bit later Brax reappeared. Then Elsie and little Winifred departed while Pinto scrubbed himself in the lukewarm, halfway muddied water.

"Ma said I can heat up another kettle," Ben offered as he observed Pinto's reaction to the tepid bathwater.

"It's jus' fine, Ben," Pinto insisted. "'Mos' as fine as de company."

By and by those weeks passed at the Oakes place in Wise County etched themselves into Pinto's heart. He tried telling himself Tully would be back from Kansas soon and find little use for a hireling. And there was the call of the open sky and the windswept plain, too. But at night, sitting in the loft swapping tales with Ben and Brax, Pinto Lowery found a piece of himself he thought he'd lost back in Pennsylvania when Jamie Haskell fell.

"You tell stories just fine," Ben proclaimed.

"Used to tell my cousins," Pinto said, remembering. "And come summer, when we could skin out on our chores some, I'd run off with my friends to de river bottoms and swap a few lies."

"Ain't all o' them stories lies, is they?" Brax asked.

"No, sir," Pinto declared. "Dere's particles o' truth in every one."

Better still were mornings and evenings when Pinto took his meals with the family. Elsie was a rare wonder of a cook, and she near had the flesh Pinto had run off in a season's mustanging back on his ribs. He'd almost forgotten what real coffee tasted like, and Elsie was forever putting a platter of biscuits and a tub of butter on the sideboard for him to mix with slices of jerked beef.

Fer a job a man's paid fer, dis watchin' over Elsie and the youngsters's got to be marked down at de top o' my lis', Pinto thought.

But with three-fourths of the male population of Wise County driving cattle to Kansas, some took notice. Not all came to see women and children through the steaming June afternoons. Many arrived with larceny in their hearts. Big Nose Joe Hannigan was among the worst.

It was Jared Richardson first brought word of Hannigan's arrival in Wise County.

"Thought to warn you," the young man told Pinto late one afternoon. "Didn't want to worry anybody, but we had some trouble day 'fore yesterday with some visitors."

"Oh?" Pinto asked.

"Come ridin' up to the house, screamin' like Comanches and demandin' our money. All they got fer their trouble was a load o' buckshot courtesy o' Arabella's twelve gauge. That sort o' discouraged 'em."

"I'd judge it did," Pinto said, grinning at the notion.

"Well, they went and set fire to the bunkhouse and shot up our chickens some. Scared Jim and Job considerable. Worse part's they sailed into Defiance, guns blazin', and robbed the bank. After that, they took both saloons and the mercantile."

"How many were they?" Pinto asked nervously.

"Seven to begin with," Jared explained. "Harry Allen over at the mercantile kilt one 'fore they shot him dead. They gunned ole Miz Pegram, too, who only come in to buy some gingham cloth. And a crazy kid outside the Lucky Seven Saloon got murdered, too."

The picture of a grinning face flashed through Pinto's brain, and he grew cold.

"Boy wasn't even doin' anything!" Jared exclaimed. "Shot him for the sport."

"Who was it did de shootin'?" Pinto asked.

"Young fellow, as I heard it," Jared explained. "But it's his brother's got folks boltin' their doors. Big fellow with a busted nose."

"Joe Hannigan," Pinto muttered.

"You heard o' him then?"

"Yeah, I heard o' him. It's bad luck's blew him here, and that's certain."

"Thought you ought to know. Some men tracked 'em a ways. Lost the trail just west o' here."

"And you rode out here by yerself?" Pinto cried. "Won't get old takin' chances with yer hide, boy! Bes' I see you home safe."

"No, don't you worry over me," Jared argued. "I'm smoke on

the wind out here. I know every prickly pear and brier in all o' Wise County. You look out yourself. Ain't much to stop Joe Hannigan from payin' you a visit. He's got plenty o' food from the mercantile, but he'll be needin' water. If he turns shy o' the creek, I expect he'll see your cook smoke."

"Could be," Pinto confessed.

"You could bring Miz Oakes and the little ones out to our place. We'd enjoy the company, and those outlaws ain't likely to come lookin' for more buckshot."

"Wouldn't bank on that, Jared," Pinto declared. "These men got memories."

"But there's nobody here to hold 'em off!"

"Dere's me," Pinto pointed out.

"Not much when you put it against six killers."

"Guess it'll have to be 'nough," Pinto said, sighing. "Now you bes' ride along home, Jared. I thank you fer de news, but I got no time to bury neighbors jus' now. Vamoose."

Pinto waved the young man along, then made his way solemnly toward the barn. Ben and Brax were busy toting well water to the house, and Pinto joined them for a moment. Once inside, he pointed to a shotgun resting over the door.

"Know how to fire her?" Pinto asked.

"That's Ma's gun," Ben explained. "But there's a Springfield in the cupboard I fired lots o' times."

"Well, you leave de shotgun to her then," Pinto said, scratching his chin. It was hard to imagine prim and proper Elsie Oakes firing a load of buckshot at anybody. "You see riders come, you take out that rifle and be ready. You shoot any strangers come callin', hear?"

"Expectin' trouble?" Brax asked excitedly. "That what Jared rode out to say?"

"Was," Pinto admitted.

"Was what?" Elsie asked, stepping over to join them.

"Trouble," Pinto explained. "Wors' kind." He then motioned her outside and related the tale of Big Nose Joe Hannigan.

* * *

Pinto Lowery had never been a man to wait for trouble to come calling. No, he believed in meeting a thing head on. After satisfying himself Elsie understood the peril and insisting the children stay close to home till the danger passed, Pinto saddled the black and prepared to track down the Hannigans.

"You ain't goin' for good, are you, Pinto?" Brax asked.

"Lef' my blanket roll in de lof', didn't I?" Pinto responded. "I'll be along in a bit. Tomorrow. Or maybe de day after."

"I could go with you," Ben offered.

"You got a job," Pinto told the youngster. "And I got one, too."

Thereupon he set off to locate the Hannigans.

Joe Hannigan had ridden the outlaw trail often enough to know the difference between real danger and a pack of farmboys and saloon owners out to get some bank money back. Pinto supposed the Hannigan gang spent a whole hour losing their pursuers. Currently the bandits were camped just above a winding creek west of the Trinity River. Big Nose Joe and his brother Pat were splashing in the shallows with two youthful-looking companions. The other two outlaws kept watch from the hillside.

Pinto drank it all in from the far side of the creek. A stand of locusts offered good shelter there. He'd left the black fifty yards back in a narrow ravine. Best not to alert a nervous lookout, and a restless stallion was apt to stir or whine any moment.

For close to an hour Pinto watched the swimmers. Eventually Pat spelled the guards, who then took to the water. It was a terrible temptation for Pinto. One bullet through the forehead of Pat Hannigan, and the outlaws would be helpless before the barrel of the Henry. It wasn't half so hard a shot as others Pinto had made. Still, a miss spelled death, and killing the whole gang would be less than likely.

Ain't got de stomach for it anymore, Pinto thought. At Fredericksburg he and Jamie Haskell had stood there firing round after round into the surging blueshirted mass coming up the heights.

Whole companies had been cut down. What were six men to the thousands?

It's different when you can see their faces, Pinto told himself. And no matter what they had done, Pinto Lowery lacked the anger to boil his blood.

It was later, toward nightfall, that Pat Hannigan took out a mouth organ and started playing haunting tunes.

"Joe, that noise'll carry for miles," one of the gang complained. "Sure to draw that posse."

"Maybe they'll bring that girl and her shotgun," Pat said between tunes. "Eh, Joe?"

The big-nosed killer scowled and kicked a rock into the creek.

"Might be I'll swing back that way and visit that gal," Joe growled. "As for a posse, I almost welcome 'em. It's gotten too fool quiet hereabouts for my likin'. In the old days, you could depend on a Comanche to make a try for yer horse or some farmer to happen along. Nowadays you got to ride into town to find any excitement."

"Hard to stay long when you rob the place," Pat observed. "Wish I'd got a bottle 'fore you shot that pup outside the saloon."

"He got in my way," Joe grumbled.

"Well, he didn't learn much from his mistake," a sandy-haired outlaw said, laughing.

"Try another tune," Joe suggested, and Pat struck up a melody.

The music plagued Pinto near as much as the conversation. As the Hannigans told stories of this outrage or that, Pinto fumed. It was bad enough to hear such talk, but listening to the mouth organ brought back Muley's face.

Be nightmares dis night, Pinto knew.

Then there was the matter of the boy. What was his name? Pinto didn't even recall. Nobody would trouble themselves much about it, either. What a sad thought it was to imagine the poor kid tossed in a hole without even a marker for remembering!

Eventually Pinto lay back against a boulder and tried to catch a bit of sleep. The outlaws were resting in their blankets, and the intervening creek promised continued concealment. Even so, Pinto never slept more than half an hour at a time. Too many ghosts haunted his dreams.

Come daybreak the Hannigans began breaking camp. They did so in no great hurry, and more than once Pinto thought to fetch help and take the killers then and there. He dared not leave them to visit the Oakes place, though.

Joe Hannigan made his way to the creek and drew out a razor. As Hannigan soaped his face, Pinto thought of the day poor Muley had begged the use of Pinto's strap.

"Got my pa's old razor," the boy had said. "Just need to put an edge on it."

"And to grow some whiskers," Elmer Tubbs had said, laughing. "Now get to work you no-account!"

No-account? Pinto thought. The boy was worth a dozen Elmer Tubbses.

That was when Pinto saw the watch fob. Joe Hannigan twirled it in one hand while slicing off the beginnings of a beard with a razor held in the other. Pinto Lowery recalled that fob. Elmer Tubbs was partial fond of it. He'd held it himself the day Pinto had ridden away.

So, Tubbs, you caught up with 'em, did you? Wasn't the first fool to rush to his death. Faye and the youngsters would have a hard time of it now.

"Joe, ain't you ever gettin' finished down there?" Pat finally shouted.

"Didn't know you to be in such a rush," Joe answered.

"Ain't generally," Pat admitted. "Got a feelin', though. Feel better when I put this place behind me."

"Gone seein' omens in the clouds like Pa?"

"No, but there's somethin' just the same."

Joe finished his shave and wiped his face clean. He was preparing to climb the hill when one of the younger outlaws let loose a howl.

"Lord, Jimmy, what's got you befuddled?"

"This!" the young outlaw exclaimed, pulling a small object from his saddlebag. "What is it, Joe?"

"Oh, that," Pat said, laughing as he tossed something to his big brother.

"Why it's ears, boy," Joe explained, tossing them back. "Cut off that freight boy back in Doan's Creek."

"Ears!" Jimmy cried.

"We took fingers once," Joe explained. "Makes a man think hard 'fore he takes to followin'."

"And you cut 'em off him live?" a horrified bandit asked.

"This time," Joe explained. "Mostly the fool's already dead, though. Take that boy in Defiance."

The words bore into Pinto's soul like fire brands. Without thinking he raised the old Henry and took aim. At the last minute Joe Hannigan knelt over to pick up the ears, though, and Pinto's bullet missed the big-nosed villain and splintered the cheekbone of a younger outlaw at his side.

"Coley?" Pat yelled as the young bandit clasped his face and rolled his eyes back into his head. Then the knees buckled. The outlaw died before he hit the ground.

"Over across the creek there!" Joe yelled, ducking behind his horse.

Pinto paid it little mind. He was angry now, full of fury. He scanned the hillside and located each outlaw in turn. Mostly they kept to cover. Jimmy, though, made a run for his rifle. Pinto fired, and the Henry sent a round slicing into the young raider's side and down into his insides. Jimmy threw back his arms and clawed the air.

"Best we bring him along, Joe," Pat said, inching his way toward the wounded man.

"No need," Joe said, firing a pistol ball through Jimmy's head. "Only slow us down. Get mounted. Let's put some space 'tween us and that there posse."

Pinto fired twice more, but the Hannigan gang moved quickly. In an instant it seemed they were atop horses and riding north. They left the better part of their camp behind. What did that matter? They'd only steal what they needed later.

"Leas'wise dey gone north," Pinto muttered. The Oakes place was south. It was in that direction that Pinto Lowery turned.

Chapter 9

After his encounter with the Hannigans, Pinto never again slept soundly in the loft of the Oakes barn. Even the slightest sound brought him rushing to the loft window, Henry rifle at the ready. Word came that the Hannigans were raiding Chickasaw trading posts up in the Nations and robbing stagecoaches in Kansas. To others Big Nose Joe was a distant threat at best. For Pinto the broken-nosed bandit lurked in every shadow.

Elsie took note of his unease and quizzed him about it.

"It's not somethin' the children've done, I hope," she said. "Ben and Brax can be awful pests, and Winnie's forever carryin' on about the chickens or some such nonsense. It must be tiresome to a man."

"Is it tiresome fer you, ma'am?" Pinto asked.

"I fear I'm used to it."

"Me, I'm not," Pinto confessed. "See, de thing is, a man can get pure tired o' what he's used to. It's de fresh times keep him alive. Hate to confess it, but I gone and got real fond o' dem youngsters. Feels like fambly almos'. Be missin' it when yer man gets back and I ride back onto de Llano."

"Haven't you ever considered starting a family of your own, Pinto?"

"Pondered many a thing. But I been wanderin' too long. Too many wild ways in me fer a woman to tame."

"You make it sound like breakin' a mustang."

"Ain't it jus' so? Way I figure things, a horse'd be easy compared to gentlin' a stubborn ole cuss like me."

She laughed at the words. Then she rested a hand on his shoulder. It remained but an instant, and thereafter Elsie hurried to get her washing done. Pinto watched her with a perplexed look on his face. Then he, too, set off to tend his chores.

Summers weren't entirely to be spent working, though. Pinto had told his mother that often enough. As he slaved away in the cornfields, thinning plants under a blistering June sun, he recognized the first traces of despair creeping across the faces of his young helpers. Neither Ben nor Brax were of a size to long endure heavy toil, and Pinto brought that fact to Elsie's attention.

"Don't you figure I know it's wearin' 'em down?" she asked angrily. "How else's the work to get done, Pinto? Tully and Truett aren't back yet, and if the plants aren't thinned, they'll not a one of 'em grow a proper ear. Soon we'll have to tote water to 'em as well. Farmin's not an easy life. For man or boy. Next year we'll have Winnie out there, too. And as it is, she works half the day helpin' me with washin', cookin', and tendin' the garden."

"Didn't mean to complain," Pinto apologized. "Was only thinkin' a spot o' swimmin', maybe some noontime fishin', even a hunt, jus' might raise some spirits."

"Fresh meat would be welcome enough," Elsie admitted. "We've eaten about as many of the chickens as we dare. I thought to butcher a hog, but with Tully not accounted for, best we save the hogs against winter need."

"He'll be along 'fore long," Pinto reassured her. "Ole Richardson was haulin' a fair number o' pitiful critters. He'll be givin' 'em time to fatten up for sellin'."

"I'm certain you're right," she said. "Still, it does give cause for a hunt. Tru and Jared Richardson shot a pair of wild pigs up near the river crossin' in April. Fair number of 'em, to hear Tru talk of it."

"Shot myself a javelina once," Pinto said, scratching his chin. "Was eleven. Javelina's a sort o' wild hog."

"I know," Elsie said, smiling. "I was born and reared in Texas, Pinto. These pigs down on the river don't have tusks, though. I'd guess they wandered off some abandoned farm durin' one of the Indian scares."

"Not much to sing about, shootin' a pig without tusks," Pinto muttered. "But I'd guess de meat'll be tasty jus' de same."

"We'll turn it slow, on a spit over a bed of coals. Basted with honey."

"Can already smell it," Pinto said, nodding. "Bes' I get a pair o' boys and set about shootin' it. Elsewise smellin's all we'll be doin'."

And so early the next morning Pinto led Ben and Brax out toward the Trinity. Ben's shoulders sagged beneath the weight of the ancient Springfield rifled musket, a relic of the war. Pinto wasn't sure a man could hit what he aimed for with the piece since the rifling was worn nigh smooth, and the hammer didn't always strike the cap quite right.

"Tru took it into Defiance when a travelin' gunsmith come through," Ben had explained. "Man said twenty Yankee dollars'd fix it just fine. That was the price he was askin' fer one o' those new Winchesters."

Pinto had laughed. If he had the chance, he'd let Ben have a turn at the Henry.

They came upon the first traces of the pigs near a shallow bend just upstream from where the Decatur road crossed the West Fork of the Trinity. There was a considerable wallow there, and several runs torn in the underbrush beyond.

"I know pig leavin's when I see 'em," Ben declared. "Ain't I shoveled enough o' their dung into Ma's garden?"

"Me, I don't have to see it," Brax remarked. "I can smell pig."

“’Less you can call ’em to you, bes’ quiet down,” Pinto urged. “Pigs ain’t altogether senseless. Dey got ears.”

The three hunters started cautiously into the underbrush. Pinto had seen a boy lamed by a javelina sow once. Big mama hog just bent that boy’s leg back and snapped it above the knee. Wild or tame, a hog wasn’t a creature to trifle with. The Oakes boys knew that, and they kept a sharp lookout for trouble. But it was Pinto who first spied the pigs.

They’d made themselves to home in a nest of boulders. It was a regular pig town, with mamas and papas and plenty of little squeakers.

“Don’t shoot the mama hog,” Brax whispered as Pinto readied his rifle. “She’s got babies.”

“They all got babies,” Ben objected.

“Shhh,” Pinto pleaded.

“That ’un,” Brax said, pointing to a young boar intent on quarreling with some elder. Pinto half smiled. Then he steadied the Henry and fired.

The rifle knocked the pig a foot in the air and threw it down, dead. Ben swung the Springfield toward a big sow, but Pinto shook his head.

“Here,” Pinto said, waving Ben over while the pigs whined and squealed. The mustanger helped the twelve-year-old aim the Henry. Then Ben pressed the trigger, and the sow fell over on one shoulder and died.

“I didn’t want to kill the mamas,” Brax grumbled as a piglet raced down the run.

“I couldn’t tell from thirty yards away,” Ben explained. “All I knew was to pick out a big ’un.”

The two boys set to arguing, and Pinto left them behind. He tended to the throat cuts, then hacked a branch off a willow.

“What you doin’, Pinto?” Ben called.

“Makin’ a drag fer de pigs,” Pinto answered. “Can’t do de butcherin’ here. See about tearin’ some yucca into strips. We’ll weave us a thatch.”

"A what?" Brax asked.

"Thatch," Pinto said, tearing a yucca strip and showing the boys how to make a mat.

Ben said, grinning, "Sometimes we can hardly figure out what you're sayin', Pinto. All that muddle o' East Texas talk. Pa says East Texans talk like they got mush in their mouths."

"Ain't how a man talks's important," Pinto declared. "It's what he says."

"Maybe," Ben agreed. "But it does help considerable if you can tell what he did say."

They went on bantering back and forth for a quarter hour. By then the drag was finished, and Pinto hauled the bloody pigs over and tossed them onto the yucca mat.

"Time we headed back," Pinto announced.

"Not without us havin' a swim," Ben argued. "Ma said we could. I asked her."

"Me, too," Brax added. "You need a wash, anyhow. Got blood all over you."

"Yeah, I got some on me," Ben noted. "My kill."

"Sure, a poor sow," Brax grumbled.

"It'll taste mighty good, won't it, Pinto?"

"You boys goin' to quarrel or swim?" Pinto asked as he sat on the bank and pulled off his boots. In seconds the youngsters managed to peel off their clothes and splash into the Trinity. By the time Pinto joined them, they were ready and met him with a wall of water. He was half an hour getting his revenge.

"How's it feel, killin' somethin'?" Brax asked later when the three of them sat on the bank drying.

"Ain't like you'd think," Ben volunteered. "Not excitin' exactly. Kind of cold, somehow. I felt like askin' that pig to forgive me."

"Not altogether a bad notion," Pinto observed. "Indians say prayers 'fore dey start a hunt. Ask de animals to give 'emselves up so de people can live."

"I think I'm doin' that from now on," Ben declared.

"Do you figure they do that when they hunt men?" Brax asked.

"Comanches kilt Grandpa Oakes. Figure they prayed first?"
"They didn't eat Grandpa," Ben muttered.
"Killin' men's different," Pinto told the boys.
"How?" Ben asked.
"You kilt men, ain't you, Pinto?"
"In de war," Pinto answered. "Mos'ly, though, we jus' shot off our rifles with everybody else. You never knew fer sure you killed a man or not. Twice, though, I fired right at a fellow. Firs' was a tall one with a big mustache. Second one was only a boy, no bigger'n a flea. But he had his rifle, so I couldn't do anything else'n drop him."
"It was war," Ben said, offering a reassuring nod.
"Been times since, too," Brax said, scowling.
"Three of 'em," Pinto confessed. "On de trail to Wichita I dropped a raider. Den I come to be Comanche charged."
"And the other?" Brax asked.
"Don't much remember," Pinto lied.
"We know 'bout it," Ben whispered. "Jared came by to say the Defiance posse come across two men out past Willingham Creek. Said they happened to be Hannigan cousins."
"How you figure I did it?" Pinto asked.
"They found Henry casings across the river," Ben explained. "And some tracks."
"I heard about them Hannigans," Brax said, inching closer to Pinto. "Will they come to our place?"
"Might," Pinto admitted. "I hear dey went up Kansas way."
"Pa's there," Ben pointed out. "And Tru."
"I'm afraid," Brax said, resting his head on Pinto's shoulder.
"No point to that, Brax," Pinto argued. "Man faces life as he comes across her, a day at a time. Nothin' else he can do."
"Ain't easy when you're ten," Ben said, rising and drawing his brother over.
"Nor when yer older," Pinto told them. "But it's what needs doin'."
They set about getting dressed then, and afterward hauled the

pigs back to the farm. Pinto skinned the beasts and tacked the hides to the barn wall. He butchered the meat and took it to Elsie. She already had Ben and Brax building up a fire, so Pinto headed back to drag the carcasses away from the house.

They were most of the day cooking the meat, and it was near nightfall when they finally had their feast. Pinto gnawed ribs like there was no tomorrow, and the boys seemed to eat their weight. Even little Winnie gobbled away.

"I fear we were more in need of fresh meat than I'd imagined," Elsie declared when even Ben admitted he was full.

"Well, we've all o' us been workin' hard," Pinto observed. "Body needs somethin' solid in him now and again."

"Like half a pig?" Brax asked, laughing.

"Didn't see you passin' up any ribs, Brax," Pinto said, and Winnie giggled her agreement as Ben gave his brother a halfhearted poke.

That was when Pinto first heard the intruders. His face paled, and the others noticed. Instantly silence befell the farm.

"There," Ben said, pointing toward the barn door.

"And there!" Brax said, shrinking back toward his mother as he pointed toward a shadow beside the woodpile.

"Res' easy," Pinto said, throwing a fresh log on the fire. "Elsie, maybe Ben can help you to get de food put by. Brax, you take Winnie along."

"Ben, fetch the meat," Elsie instructed. "I'll get the shotgun."

"No, you stay inside," Pinto urged. "Ain't work fer a shotgun."

The rising flames illuminated the first of the visitors slinking beside the barn door. A second and third followed, and Brax was right about the one by the woodpile. Pinto drew out his pistol and watched them turn toward the fire.

"Wolves!" Brax shouted from the doorway. "Pinto, come on."

"Not wolves," Pinto declared as he read the starvation in the poor beasts' eyes. They'd been drawn by the carcasses and had surely picked them clean. Now half-satisfied hunger drove them to try for more.

"It's jus' some poor ole farm dogs," Pinto announced. "Maybe run off a place like dem pigs. Gone wild."

"Pinto, come along inside!" Elsie shouted. "Wolf or dog, they'll chew you down to the bone if given half a chance."

"We'll throw 'em some meat!" Ben suggested.

"You do, and they'll be here every night," Pinto explained. "Get!" he shouted, firing off the first two chambers of his pistol. The dogs drew back, uttering low growls. Then one of them made a charge at Pinto. The Colt turned to meet the threat. A yellow flash exploded from the pistol, and the dog whimpered and fell.

"More?" Pinto asked.

The dogs seemed to understand. One and then another slipped away.

"They gone?" Ben finally asked.

"Seems so," Pinto answered. "Get me a spade, Ben. Bes' I bury that dog 'fore dey come back to eat it."

Chapter 10

It was mid-July when Truett Oakes appeared between the waist-high stalks of corn plants in the fields beyond the house. Pinto couldn't help grinning as he watched Ben and Brax rush over to their brother and pull him from the saddle. The three boys rolled into a ball, crushing plants and raising dust for a quarter hour. Then Truett kicked his way free.

"Ben, figure you can tend my horse?" the elder Oakes asked.

"Sure," Ben agreed. "But we got plants left to thin."

"Seems to me we thinned enough of 'em," Truett said, pointing to the trampled stalks. "Brax, maybe you can collect the tools and come along later."

"I can," Brax replied with a grin.

Truett glanced but a moment at Pinto. There was something unspoken on the fourteen-year-old's face.

"Comin', Pinto?" Ben asked as he took Truett's horse and started for the barn.

"No need him quittin' early," Truett said sharply. "We got some family business to tend."

They walked perhaps ten feet when Pinto overheard Brax ask, "Where's Pa?"

* * *

Pinto had a nose for knowing when and where he was wanted, and he judged right that at the moment he was neither one where Truett Oakes was concerned. It didn't take any great notion of sense to tell something had happened to Tully. A man wouldn't send his boy riding home alone across that stretch of country without a good reason. Pinto counted a hundred ways you could snap a leg or take fever between Wise County and Kansas, and there were just as many lurking on the way home.

"Bes' to stay here and leave 'em to have their talk," Pinto told himself. "Dey'll fetch me if I'm needed."

The summons wasn't long in coming. Little Winnie ran out and clasped Pinto's hand.

"Ma said to bring you to the house, Pinto," the little girl explained. "Somethin's happened to Pa."

Pinto nodded somberly and hurried to keep pace with Winifred's flying feet. In no time they were sitting on the porch on one side of Elsie. The three boys were on the other.

"I don't see why he's here," Truett growled. "This is for family to decide."

"Pinto's mostly family," Ben argued.

"He's kept us safe while you were away, Truett," Elsie said. "And what's happened effects him, too. You haven't forgotten we owe him money."

"Here!" Truett shouted, tearing a money belt from his ribs and flinging it at Elsie's feet. "Here's money. Plenty of it. Mr. Richardson gave me full wages for the both of us. Steer money's there, too. Ain't much by way of replacement, though."

"No, it's not," Elsie admitted. "Still, it's no call to shout at your mother or to act uncivil toward friends. Whether you believe it or not, I number Mr. Lowery among the very best friends we've known."

"Excuse me, ma'am," Pinto said, rising. "I wouldn't bring a family trouble, not when it seems to have a fair slice already. I'll be over to de barn."

"Stay," Elsie insisted. "We need your counsel."

"We do not!" Truett objected. "It's for me to decide things."

"What things?" Elsie cried. "Who your brothers will live with? What charitable aunt or cousin will take Winnie in? Without this farm we won't be able to feed them."

"Cousin Ryan's made a fair offer," Truett argued. "With that money we could buy . . ."

"What?" his mother asked. "A shop where I could take in washin'? We're a long way from givin' up this land. Before any of you boys could walk, Tully and I were makin' a go of it here. I see no reason to sell our home!"

"But Pa was the one saw to the plowin'," Truett declared. "Was him did the heavy work. I promised him I'd take care of things. I'm the man here now."

"You're little more than a boy, even if your heart's as big as Texas. You don't know town life. I do," Elsie said, lifting Truett's chin. "We've made do half the summer with you and your father both gone. It's an extra hand we've added, don't you see?"

For a moment a world of silence rained down on them. Grief and confusion muted the children. Elsie had begun to tremble, and Truett was red-faced angry.

"What's happened?" Pinto finally asked, hoping to break the spell.

"It's Pa," Ben whimpered.

"Happened the second week out," Truett explained. "In the Nations. Pa's horse found a gopher hole and pitched him off. Landed funny. A rib broke off and went through both lungs. Died spittin' blood and callin' out how I should take care of everybody.

"We dug him a hole 'neath a cottonwood, and I carved his name in the side so folks'd know he come that way."

"Hard trail, that 'un," Pinto muttered.

"Next day raiders hit us. Shot Brent Lee all to pieces. Left him to be trampled by the cattle so there was hardly anything left to bury. Cousin Ryan hauled him back to the cottonwood so Pa'd have the company."

"Pa favored Brent," Elsie said, swallowing hard.

"There's worse news I ain't told you," Truett added. "Half the stolen steers were ours. And we didn't get top price for the ones we sold in Wichita. Still, if we pooled that with what's been offered on the farm, we could buy a mercantile store, or maybe open up a roomin' house in Decatur. You said yourself, Ma, it's shameful how shy that town is of places to put up."

"It takes work to make a go of anything," Elsie said, sighing. "What sounds to you like an answer's only the worst kind of gamble. I don't know anything about shopkeeping, and a rooming house wants boarders. If it hasn't any, what do you do? Here we have corn to grind, vegetables in the garden, and fresh meat for winter."

"There's huntin' and fishin', too," Ben pointed out. "Maybe Pinto'll show us how to rope mustangs."

"He ain't stayin'!" Truett barked. "Wouldn't be proper with Pa just dead to have a man around."

"He's owed wages," Elsie said, trembling as she tried to grasp the money belt.

"I'll count it out," Truett offered. "Plus ten dollars extra for your trouble."

"Didn't ask fer that," Pinto said, accepting only the promised wages. "One thing's bes' learned early, too. Dollars ain't de bes' way to repay a man fer troublin' himself. Dip o' de hat and a handshake's more fittin' wage."

Winnie crawled over and hugged Pinto's side, and he lifted her onto one shoulder and smiled.

"Squared us, I figure," the grizzled mustanger declared as he smiled at the girl. He then returned Winnie to her mother and turned to leave.

"You can't go," Elsie objected. "We've got harvest to get in, and there's . . ."

"Boy's jus' worried after what folks'd whisper," Pinto replied. "I'm no farmhand. Be plenty o' young hands'll want work now they come back from Kansas. I never figured to stay all summer anyhow."

"You can't just leave!" Elsie argued.

"Never was one fer long good-byes," Pinto told her. Ben and Brax raced over and blocked his departure, but Pinto easily lifted one and then the other out of the way and continued.

"No," Brax said, wrapping himself around one arm and pulling with all his might. "Not 'fore supper. Ain't it enough Pa's not come back?"

Pinto lifted the ten-year-old into the air and tried to shake him free. That was when the tears began. A man that roamed the Llano, who'd fought with Bob Lee and outfoxed Comanches, grew a hardness. But Pinto Lowery's resolve melted at the touch of those tears.

"Stay to supper," Ben pleaded. "Maybe the night. I expect we'll all of us need a story."

"Please," Elsie called from the porch.

Pinto turned and looked Truett Oakes in the eye. It was up to Tru.

"Guess one night wouldn't hurt," Truett grumbled. "Long's you head off early tomorrow."

"Can leave right now if it's what you want."

"Ain't," Ben announced, gazing hard at his elder brother. "Is it, Tru?"

"You're welcome to stay as long as you choose, Pinto," Elsie declared. "Isn't he, Truett?"

"Don't see how a day or so'd hurt," the boy mumbled. "Sure." But any fool could see the young man didn't mean it.

Chapter 11

There was very little cheer in the Oakes house that night. Elsie did her best to bolster spirits by baking a pair of chickens and adding generous portions of fresh greens, together with mounds of potatoes. No one had much appetite, though. As it dawned on the little ones that their father wouldn't be coming back, more than a few tears crossed cheeks. Elsie herself wasn't much better. She pulled an old rocker out onto the porch and drew Winnie up on one knee. For a time the two of them hummed an old lullaby. Later they only rocked.

Pinto left them to their grief. He hadn't even eaten at the table. Instead he'd filled a plate and taken it out past the well. The corral was nearby, and presently he found his white-faced stallion better company than the family he'd taken too much to heart.

"Wish I knew somethin' to say or do," he whispered to the horse. "But I don't suppose de words ever got put down that'd give a boy much peace when his pa dies. Nor fer Elsie."

Later Ben came out and took the empty plate.

"Maybe a walk to de creek'd help," Pinto suggested.

"Thanks, Pinto, but I ain't got much interest. Ma said to stick close tonight, and Tru said we're sure to have nightmares. He did himself. Brax just lies on his bed and cries."

"Could be it's bes'. Cryin' can loosen up de hurt, let it work its way out o' you."

"You don't understand," Ben said, shuddering. "It's not like cryin' over a stillborn colt or a broken leg. It's Pa's gone and died. Pa! He was bigger'n stronger'n anybody I ever knew. How's it possible?"

"Hard times," Pinto muttered. "Things go and happen. Who can tell how come? You got some memories o' yer pa. Hold 'em close. Share 'em with Brax 'cause he won't remember so good as you do."

"You don't forget your pa," Ben insisted.

"Don't if you ever knew him," Pinto said, sighing. "Me, I recall some uncles and my ma o' course, but as to a pa, I jus' have what I got told. And I do remember a yellow tintype. Not much to help you get yer growin' done."

"You didn't have a pa, Pinto?"

"Oh, I guess I had one, sure enough. But he died when I was jus' a sprout, accordin' to what Ma told me."

"Who taught you to rope and ride? Who showed you how to hold a razor? Or shoot a gun?"

"Cousins mos'ly. Friends. Shoot, was a preacher fellow up in Virginia give me my first shavin' lesson. Me and Jamie Haskell, the both o' us. Near carved my chin off!"

Pinto laughed at the recollection, and for a moment Ben forgot his pain. The boy's frown returned directly, though, and Pinto couldn't come by a single word to erase it.

"Best I get back to the house now," Ben finally said. "Maybe you'd give us a story later on."

"Give her a try," Pinto promised.

"You'll be up in the loft?" Ben asked. Pinto nodded, and the boy scratched his chin. "Maybe I can even talk Tru into comin'. He might share a tale or two he picked up ridin' to Kansas."

"That'd be fine," Pinto declared.

"Brax'll come anyway," Ben said as he headed toward the house. "And me!"

But later when Pinto sat in the piled hay in the barn loft, staring through the open window at the moon glowing above, he didn't really expect company. Then when he heard footsteps on the ladder, he knew they belonged to Ben and Brax. Death and turmoil had aged Truett past stories.

"Settle in close," Pinto urged as he made room for a youngster on each side of him. "I ain't told dis tale in a bit, and las' time it near scared my pants off. As fer de boys that was there, was one soiled his trousers."

"Did not," Brax said, shaking his head. "Men're always sayin' that when they want to scare somebody."

"Well, I'll leave de story to do de scarin'," Pinto answered. And so he launched into the tale of Cannonball Elton, the Confederate corporal beheaded by a federal cannoneer. Poor Elton was floating over the Petersburg trench line, howling and screaming as he looked for his head, and the Oakes boys were attaching themselves to Pinto's side, when a different sort of shriek had the three of them jumping into the air.

"What was that?" Ben screamed.

"Was Cannonball!" Brax cried, hugging Pinto's side.

"No, it wasn't," Pinto said, prying Brax loose and crawling over to where the Henry rested in a blanket. "Get down, boys! Ain't you never heard a Comanche?"

Instantly a new fear gripped the youngsters. Brax burrowed his way into the straw. Ben rushed for the ladder.

"Got to get to Ma," Ben explained.

"Stay where you be," Pinto ordered. "You go runnin' down dere, yer ma's apt to shoot yer fool head off. Watch de barn door. May be dem visitors'll sneak in behind us. I got to keep an eye on de house."

"Ma's there!" Ben argued.

"So's her shotgun," Pinto pointed out. "I expec' she'll know what to do with it."

Pinto, meanwhile, edged his way to the large loft window and studied the ground below. A pair of skulking figures approached the corral. Pinto's black backed nervously and reared its forelegs at a slight-shouldered raider.

"They're after your horse," Brax said, crawling over beside Pinto. "Look there!"

A second Indian climbed the corral rails while a third made a run at the house. Pinto aimed the Henry over their heads and discharged a shot at each. The Comanches in the corral flattened themselves and shouted angrily toward the well. The small figure racing toward the house continued on. As he flung open the door, Elsie's shotgun blew him back into the yard.

"Lord, he's blown to pieces," Brax said, hiding his eyes.

"Is Ma all right?" Ben asked, leaving his lookout post long enough to have a peek. A rifle spit yellow flame from the well at the loft then, and the bullet sliced a splinter from the window frame an inch from Ben's shoulder.

"Get down, fool boy!" Pinto shouted. He then watched the well, and when a shadowy shoulder slid off to one side, Pinto fired. His bullet struck the raider low, and he howled in pain. The two Comanches at the corral dashed to the aid of their friend and helped him limp away. One returned and tried to swing open the corral gate, but Pinto discouraged him with a close shot. The Indians shouted defiantly before creeping to their horses and riding away.

Only then did Pinto smell the smoke.

"They've fired the barn!" Ben howled.

Pinto took a final glance below, then hurried the boys down the ladder. By that time Elsie had stepped out onto the porch, and Truett was drawing a bucket of water from the well. The fourteen-year-old dashed over and splashed the water against the yellow flames licking the west wall of the barn.

"No, bes' wet some blankets," Pinto instructed as he arrived. "Never get 'nough water on it in time that way."

"Fetch 'em, Ben!" Elsie hollered, and Ben sped off toward the house. Brax followed his brother. They returned shortly with two blankets apiece. Little Winnie brought a third.

"Keep pullin' water," Pinto told Truett after dampening the first two blankets. He handed one to Elsie, and the two of them set to beating down the growing flames. In a few minutes Ben and Brax joined the work. Truett then filled buckets and wet the blankets again. Afterward he threw a bucketful into the worst of the flames when it wasn't needed to keep the blankets wet.

Pinto worked furiously. The boys and Elsie were at his side at first, but smoke and heat sent them retreating periodically. Except for flashing a look at the big black pawing the dirt of the corral, Pinto barely paused. He blamed himself for the fire, and he wasn't about to leave the Oakes family fatherless and barnless to boot.

They were close to an hour halting the fire, and another hour tearing the still-smoldering planks off the wall and drowning them proper.

"Pinto, you all right?" Ben asked when the mustanger finally dropped to his knees and coughed smoke from his lungs.

"By and by it'll pass," Pinto mumbled hoarsely. "Swallowed some smoke."

"You've burned the hair off your wrists," Elsie observed. "Ben, go fetch that goose grease."

"Later on you'll need your needle, too, Ma," Ben told her. "He's burned the right leg right off his britches."

Pinto studied his reddened knee and shook his head.

"I thank you for what you done, mister," Truett managed to say. "Was good thinkin', usin' them blankets."

"No, jus' de bad luck o' battlin' barn fires before," Pinto said, coughing again. "You live to grow older, you pick up a thing or two."

"'Course I can't say much for your shootin'," Truett added. "I swore you had that 'un by the well dead to rights."

"Lamed him," Pinto explained.

"And the ones in the corral?"

"Boys," Pinto said, spitting a black sludge from his mouth. "My ole horse had 'em buffaloed. You go to killin' Indians, you get a whole lot o' war to fight."

"Ma kilt one," Brax said, gazing back at the figure lying near the porch.

Ben stepped carefully past the corpse as he trotted over with the goose grease. Elsie treated Pinto's burns, then turned to where the little ones had gathered with Truett beside the body.

"Look at him, Ma," Brax said, warily touching a bare leg. The chest and face were bloodied by buckshot, but from the waist down it seemed here was just a splinter of a boy. "No bigger'n me," Brax added. "Wonder why he come to charge the house."

"Confused most likely," Truett said, turning the body with his toe so that the bloody horror wasn't staring up at them. "I remember we run across rustlers. I never shot at a man before, and I near ran my horse right into the middle of 'em, not knowin' better."

"I didn't see how small he was," Elsie complained. "I never would've . . ."

"That knife he's carryin' is plenty big enough," Pinto told her. "Might be he'd passed jus' eleven, twelve summers on de Llano, but that's all it takes fer a Comanche to learn to fight. Don't seem proper, gettin' killed so little, but den yer Pa fallin' off a horse ain't got much sense to it, neither."

"Come along, children," Elsie urged as she waved them toward the door. "Truett, maybe you'll . . ."

"You'll need him to help with de little 'uns," Pinto interrupted. "Trus' me to see dis 'un here's laid to res'."

"I can come back and help dig the hole," Truett offered.

"I figured do have a good look 'round anyhow," Pinto explained. "Maybe if they see he's tended, they won't see a need to come back."

"Tru?" Elsie called.

"Comin', Ma," the young man answered.

They walked together to the house, leaving Pinto alone beside the small body. Pinto wrapped the corpse in one of the smoke-blackened blankets and raised it across his weary shoulder. Strange it didn't weigh more.

He grabbed a spade and started walking. Soon he passed the barn and continued out toward the hillside beyond. When he halted, he heard a coyote howl in the distance.

"Oughtn't to be," Pinto called. "People killin' each other. Oughtn't to be!"

The howls grew silent, but there was a stirring in the grasses. It stopped when Pinto gently laid the body in the grass and began digging the grave. He hummed the melody of an old hymn as he worked, and after laying the body in the warm ground, he filled in the trench and covered it with rocks.

"Res' easy, boy," Pinto said as he touched the rocky cairn. He then turned and walked past a lurking shadow toward the barn.

Chapter 12

Pinto fell in and out of a light sleep that night. There was an eerie whine to the wind, and the recollection of that dead sliver of a Comanche boy haunted him.

"Won't be de only one, neither," Pinto muttered. He knew little Brax would be tossing anxiously. As to Elsie, well, who could know how a mother would feel looking down at another woman's slain child?

"Can't let it haunt you, Georgie," the voice of Jamie Haskell whispered in a dream. "Was the enemy, you know."

"Wasn't but a fool boy, no different'n you or me," Pinto's voice answered the phantom as it had years before in Virginia. "Jus' followin' his cap'n, same's we did. Lot o' fool boys bound to die 'long dese Virginia rivers, Jamie. Lot of 'em."

Well, a lot of Comanches had already died, and the rest were doomed to extinction, to hear the soldiers up at Fort Richardson tell it. Was a hard thing, losing your home, your friends, even your own heart. It's what happened when you came out on the short end of a war. Pinto Lowery knew.

* * *

Pinto was drifting through his netherworld of shadowy faces and stark phantoms when dawn greeted Texas the next morning. The sun didn't wake him, though. No, it took the sound of creaking rungs on the loft's ladder to do that.

"You up, Pinto?" young Ben Oakes called as he climbed. "Didn't get yourself Indian scalped durin' the night, did you?"

Pinto rubbed the fog from his eyes and glanced at Ben. The twelve-year-old peeked up at him with a mischievous grin. Pinto flung a handful of straw at the youngster and plunged his face into his blankets. It was no use, though. Brax was down below, and Winnie came trotting along shortly, cackling like a stepped-on hen.

What is it gives 'em their life? Pinto asked himself. Like as not, a kid would be flat-out spent when you needed him to husk corn. Then when you were bone-weary and needed rest, he'd take to bounding around like a spring-born calf! And these three had as fine a reason to mope as anybody ever born.

Shoot, I wasn't any different my own self, Pinto thought. He threw aside the blankets and hurried into his clothes. Then he collected his scant belongings and rolled them in the blankets.

"What'd you do that for?" Brax asked. "We cut fresh hay for the barn a bit ago, and it ought to last till harvest, don't you think?"

"It's bound to las' longer'n de need," Pinto replied. "Now Truett's back, my job's done. Time I was chasin' ponies on de Llano."

"No!" Ben objected. "You cain't go, not with Pa kilt. We need you."

"We do," Brax added, and Winnie, who had finally scaled the ladder, nodded her agreement. Pinto studied their somber faces and wished the laughter hadn't faded so quickly. He didn't like the notion his leaving would bring on sadness. There'd been enough of that already. Enough for a lifetime maybe.

"Not jus' everybody sees it that way," Pinto said at last. "'Sides, children, I'm no excuse fer a farmer."

"We raise cows, too," Ben argued. "You can teach us to be mustangers."

"Yer ma'd like that notion," Pinto said, chuckling. "Now how 'bout givin' me a hand wid this gear. Ben, you figure you can saddle my horse?"

"Get myself trampled'd be more like it. That big black don't take to me," Ben explained. "Nor to Indians."

Pinto detected a hint of a grin on Ben's face. It faded fast, though, when Pinto started down the ladder.

"Toss down my blanket roll, will you?" Pinto called when he reached the barn floor. Brax shook his head, but Ben dragged it to the lip of the loft and nudged it over the edge. Pinto caught the bundle and threw it over one shoulder. He walked out the door and turned toward the corral. After leaving his gear atop the corral rail, Pinto started back toward the barn to fetch his saddle. Elsie cut him off halfway.

"That'll wait," she hollered. "Breakfast's turnin' cold."

"Yes, ma'am," Pinto responded. Ben, Brax, and Winnie flew out of the barn, collected him, and escorted him to the house. Pinto intended taking his bacon and eggs to the porch, but Elsie insisted otherwise.

"Don't figure it's proper, Ma," Truett grumbled. "Eatin' with us. Takin' Pa's place."

"He didn't, nor will he, take your father's place!" Elsie barked. "And I swear to you, Truett Oakes, if you ever again suggest such a thing I'll whip your backside raw! It seems to me you've been entirely too free with words since your return. And you've caused injury to a man who's done nothin' to merit it. I'm sorry, Pinto. I beg your pardon."

"Only natural for him to be cross," Pinto argued. "Trail drive addles de bes' men, and de firs' one's de worse o' all."

"That's no excuse," Elsie insisted. "Truett's been taught better, and I won't have his behavior cast doubt on that fact. Tully had his faults, but being lax in his duties wasn't one of them."

"See, Tru, you've made her mad!" Ben complained. "And Pinto's talkin' about goin'."

"But you ain't really leavin'," Brax said, adding, "are you?"

"His work's done," Truett answered. "Can't keep him here forever, little brother."

"But if he'd like, he's welcome to stay on however long he wishes," Elsie declared. "Isn't he, Truett? And I believe you have other words to say, don't you?"

Truett hung his head and muttered something.

"Louder, so we can understand!" Elsie ordered.

"Was just meanin' to thank you for lookin' after things while Pa and I were off to Kansas," Truett said. "And for what you did last night . . . the fire and all. Indians, too."

"And?" Elsie prompted

"You can stay if you care. 'Course we couldn't pay, and you're sure to want to chase horses."

"Truett!"

"All I'm sayin's what everybody knows!" the fourteen-year-old replied.

Elsie prepared another lecture, but Pinto calmed the troubled waters by rising from his chair.

"I never aimed to cause a quarrel," he told them. "Bes' I get on my way now."

Truett started to reply, but Elsie hushed him. Pinto gave a departing nod to Ben and Brax, then lightly stroked Winnie's amber hair. She gripped his fingers, and he felt a powerful urge to hoist the girl onto his shoulders. Instead he lifted her chin, flashed a smile, and broke away. In five minutes' time he was busy saddling the black. Afterward he spread a blanket across the back of the packhorse and began tying down his belongings.

"Here, you best take something to eat," Elsie called as she walked toward the corral with a flour sack of food. "There's a tin of coffee, too, and cornmeal enough for johnnycakes."

"Thanks," Pinto said, accepting the sack.

"I suppose you'll be glad to be out on the open plain again," she said, sighing. "It must have been a vexation, putting up with wild boys and a pesky little girl all these weeks. Not to mention the chores. Then, too, I wish I could ride away from last night. I don't think I'll be gettin' the bloody face of that Comanche out of my dreams anytime soon."

"Wasn't anything else do do," Pinto argued. "Boys'll do such things, rushin' into early graves. By his rules, he was bein' manly, walkin' de warrior path. Dyin' young's part o' it."

"Like your friend that fell at Gettysburg?"

"I tell you 'bout him?" Pinto asked.

"Ben overheard you callin' out last night. And before, too. Is that why you won't let anyone get close?"

"What?"

"Why you won't drop your guard and let anybody care. Pinto, I've lost a husband, and I know what grief is like. I look at the boys and see Tully in their eyes, in their manners, in the way Truett stretches himself to appear taller. I cried myself to sleep last night. But I'm not stupid enough to think I can keep the pain to myself. I've got sons and a daughter to cry with, to console, to hang onto. Who have you got to share your sadness?"

"What sadness?" Pinto asked. "I get by jus' fine."

"You make a poor liar, Pinto Lowery. And you need no falsehoods here. We all know you too well. You can pretend, try to fool yourself, but it hasn't worked with us."

"I got ridin' to get done," he grumbled.

"Lord Almighty, Pinto!" she exclaimed. "I don't see why you're so determined to leave! I'm not blind, you know. It hasn't been altogether unpleasant for you here. The children are fond of you, as I think you are of them. Winnie dotes on your every glance. Brax and Ben, well, they'd follow you off a cliff. What's more, with Tully gone we need you. Stay. Help get the corn harvest in. We'll never manage it on our own."

"Sure, you will," Pinto argued. "Yer boy Truett—"

"—is full of hurt. You're needed, Pinto! Stay."

"You got to," Ben added, stepping out from behind the well. "Comanches could come back. Or even them bandits!"

"I'll ride by now and again," Pinto promised. "To see you come to no harm."

"And who's goin' to teach me things?"

"Truett will," Pinto answered. "Or you'll pick 'em up by and by like I did."

"I figured we was friends, Pinto!" Ben hollered. "You can't let Tru run you off. He don't know you. Shoot, way he figures things, a trip to Kansas makes you full grown and smart besides. Doesn't either. He'd've lost us the barn and worse, too."

"At least till we get the corn in?" Elsie pleaded.

"Couple o' months," Ben added. "Still be horses to catch."

"Pinto?" Elsie called hopefully.

"Guess you can help me strip these horses, Ben," Pinto muttered. "Only till the corn cribs're full, though. I head west thereafter."

"Sure," Ben said, rushing toward the corral, climbing the rails, and hopping down to start on the packhorse. "'Less you change your mind."

And so Pinto passed the dog days of late summer in Wise County. Mostly he devoted the time to helping the boys fill barrels with water for the near-parched cornstalks. Then, too, he sawed planks and patched the hole in the barn wall. Around midday he accompanied Ben and Brax to the river and washed away a great weariness. Truett came once or twice, but he rarely joined in the laughter and pranking unless Pinto rode off on some errand.

There were some fine times toward the end of August as harvest time neared. At least once a week Elsie packed up a food basket and brought Winnie to the fields. The whole family, which those days meant Pinto as well, had themselves a picnic under the bright summer sun. Often Elsie related some story of her ancestors, or the boys recollected a time they passed with their father.

"I miss Pa," little Winnie whimpered, and the whole gathering would sour for a minute. Ben and Brax quickly recovered, and their pranking would lift the mood. Only Truett remained downcast.

"He's slipped away," Elsie explained one evening when Pinto walked with her beside the corral. "I don't understand him anymore. He won't tell me what's botherin' him. Nor will he talk to Ben or Braxton. I worry one day he'll simply ride away as my brother Jubal did when the war started."

"He's doin' his bes' to find his own way," Pinto explained. "Won't all de words in heaven salve his wounds. Only time'll help, and it ain't been that long, you know."

"Seems an eternity."

"Sure, but it's been even longer for him. He had all those weeks on de trail wonderin' how he'd tell you. Heavy load to tote, that was."

"I know, Pinto. I just wish he'd let me lighten it some."

"Don't know that's possible, Elsie. Once a boy takes himself to be a man, ain't no turnin' back again."

"I suppose you're right. You should know if anyone."

"Yup, sure should," Pinto agreed. "You keep tryin', though. He'll come 'round. Wait and see if he don't."

Soon, though, there wasn't time to worry after Truett Oakes. The first ears of corn were maturing, and it was time to begin the harvest.

Once, back in '68, Pinto had lingered in Kansas a bit following a trail drive. He'd ridden east toward Omaha to catch a train, thus quickening the southbound journey, and he'd been surprised to see the high, straight stalks of Kansas corn. Whole yellow-green fields of the stuff, higher than a man was tall. Wise County corn, in a good year, seemed stunted. Some ears were near burnt black. But the water that had been so much effort to bring to the fields in August had brought good results to the Oakes crops.

Truett borrowed two wagons from the Double R, together with the pairs of strong-backed mules that would haul them. Elsie drove the first while young Brax guided the second. The others—Pinto, Ben, Truett, and even tiny Winnie—snapped ears off cornstalks and tossed them in the wagon beds. Clearly bushels aplenty would be taken in that year. So much, in fact, that Pinto wound up erecting three extra cribs.

"We'll sell off enough to put foldin' money by against winter need," Elsie declared jubilantly. "The rest I'll hand grind."

"You could take it to the mill up in Decatur," Truett suggested.

"They'll ask a third of the meal to do it, though," Elsie argued. "Don't have much else to keep me busy this winter. We may need more'n before. You boys are growin' like sunflowers!"

"Won't be Pa here, though," Truett muttered. "And that Lowery fellow'll be off now harvest's done."

"If he chooses to leave, he's due a share," Elsie explained.

"We didn't promise him a kernel!" Truett exploded.

"You don't have to promise friends," Elsie countered. "And you don't cheat 'em out of their due."

"Anyway, who says Pinto's leavin'?" Ben cried. "If he stayed to slave away in the fields, he's sure to want to rest up this winter. Don't you figure, Tru?"

"Who am I to know?" Truett grumbled. "Pa asked me to see to things, but nobody'll let me do it."

It took close to two weeks to get the corn in. Pinto and the boys spent half of a third week cutting stocks and hauling them to the barn for use as winter fodder. Other bundles were spread out on the range for the cattle to nibble.

"Only need feed when winter's at its worst," Ben explained to Pinto. "Mostly the cows just go on grazin' like always."

It was October when Truett again borrowed the RR wagons. It was time to take the corn to market, Elsie had decided, so the boys set to emptying the cribs into the wagon beds. Pinto couldn't help admiring Elsie's talent for turning a profit. They hauled two loads to Defiance, another two to Decatur, and then made a trip south to the thriving cowtown of Fort Worth.

Truett and Ben drove the wagons on those journeys while Pinto rode along as a guard of sorts. When Brax wasn't needed for chores, he sat alongside Ben. Mostly they drove to town, sold off the crop at the price Elsie deemed appropriate, and returned home. Only the Fort Worth trip required making camp overnight.

"If it was up to me, we'd go along home," Truett grumbled when

Pinto announced it was time to halt. "Got better'n two hours o' daylight left."

"Sure, and you could get back fine," Pinto admitted. "Dose mules'd be a while recoverin', though, and when you borrow another man's stock, it's jus' proper you show some care."

"Richardson mules are used to rough use," Truett argued. "Ain't some dandified mustang you pamper half to death."

"A horse gets fed regular and looked after some'll carry a man where he aims do go," Pinto lectured. "You use one up, you could wind up afoot when you don't much favor de prospec'."

Truett grumbled some more, but he didn't fight Pinto on the matter. Later, as dusk settled in, and the yellow-orange oak leaves on the distant hills underwent violent scarlet and amber transformation, Pinto built up a fire and began slicing a ham Elsie had sent against the need.

"I can do that," Ben offered, and Pinto turned over the chore to the yellow-haired boy.

"Rest up a bit, why don't you?" Brax added as he filled a water flask from a nearby stream. "You rode all the day, seems like. We just bounced along in the wagon."

"I'm not tired," Pinto insisted. "Shoot, sometimes I think I was born on de back of a horse. Who's to say I wasn't? I don't remember de moment any too well."

Brax laughed at the notion and began piling fresh logs onto the fire. Truett dragged the limb of a dead oak over and began cutting lengths with his ax. Those were warming sounds, the crackling of the fire and the whacking of the ax. Later, Ben whistled a tune on his mouth organ, and the three brothers took up singing.

"We used to ride out into the hills with Pa come October," Ben explained as he set a skillet atop the fire and tossed slices of ham in. "Hunted deer sometimes. Plenty o' whitetails in the Trinity bottoms."

"Jared and his pa asked if we wanted to join 'em this year," Truett said, gazing intently at the yellow flame. "I told 'em I'd happily come along. Figured you might come, too, Ben. Maybe Brax as well. Jim and Job're comin'."

"Is Pinto comin'?" Braxton asked.

"Wasn't his invite," Truett answered.

"I ain't got no rifle," Ben explained. "That ole Springfield ain't much use for huntin' deer."

"Shoots straight enough!" Truett argued. "Cousin Ryan's got a pair o' them new Winchesters, too. Said he'd bring 'em. Jared and I figured to take turns. You could have a try, too."

"Heard o' them guns, Pinto?" Brax asked.

"Fine piece," Pinto answered. "Saw one in a gunsmith shop when we sold off de crop in Decatur. Smith claimed it won't jam like my ole Henry."

"Be murder on Comanches then," Brax said, grinning as he recounted the tale Pinto had shared of the riverside fight last spring.

"Look there," Ben urged then, pointing at the darkened horizon. "Evenin' star."

"Wishin' star," Brax said adding, "Pa said so anyhow."

"Wish he was here," Truett said, creeping a hair closer to the fire.

"You know Pa knew all the names o' the stars," Ben told Pinto. "Could tell you stories 'bout 'em, too."

"Knew a man could do that," Pinto said. "Herb Granger. Used to tell us de stars was our own map. Take that big *W* over yonder."

"It's called Cassiopeia," Truett said.

"The evil queen, remember?" Ben added. "That was one o' the best stories."

"It's a good 'un to know," Pinto said, "'cause you can follow de point o' that *W* to de North Star. Follow her right up into de Chickasaw Nation, and on to Kansas."

"Canada's up there if you was to ride long enough," Ben said. "Turn 'round and you'd be in Mexico."

"Or splash into the Gulf," Truett said, grinning at the notion. "Star's not so good as a compass, but then you don't have to tote it with you."

"Have a hard time on a cloudy night, though," Ben remarked as he turned the ham slices. "Ever been to Mexico, Pinto?"

"South as far as de Nueces," Pinto replied. "Wes' to El Paso a few years back on de stagecoach. Up de trail to Kansas, o' course. Mos'ly I been eas', up Virginia way and into Pennsylvania. Durin' de war."

"Sure, we know that," Truett mumbled. "It was a long time back now. I guess you'd find Kansas pretty much changed, too."

"Hope so," Pinto responded. "Was a mean stretch o' railroad towns and angry farmers before. But den you'd know that, havin' jus' got home from de place."

"Yeah, I would," Truett agreed, straightening his posture. He then went on to describe booming Wichita for his brothers. He might have talked the whole night through had not Ben finished cooking the ham. Brax brought over a loaf of bread and some boiled eggs, and the four of them had their supper.

It was later, when they spread their blankets alongside the embers of the fire, that Pinto took charge.

"You don't want to lay yer blankets there, Brax," Pinto said as he pointed out a bed of ants. "On de upslope there aside Ben'd be better."

"I'd say," Brax agreed, laughing to himself as he stomped his boot on the ants.

"What'll we do with the ham leavin's?" Ben then asked. "I recollect them wild dogs. Wouldn't want coyotes or wolves visitin'."

"Bury those scraps," Truett suggested.

"I'll take 'em out a ways," Pinto said. "Cain't dig deeper in dis rock than a coyote'll sniff. Never knew a critter to dig at things like he will."

Pinto accepted the leavings and did as promised. On the way back he heard the boys arguing. It didn't take any great notion of intelligence to know Pinto Lowery was likely at the root of it.

"He's not Pa!" Truett exclaimed as Pinto announced his return.

"Pa's dead," Ben replied, pulling his blanket tightly against his chest.

"Warm enough?" Pinto asked. "I could toss you my saddle blanket."

"No, I'm fine," Ben assured him. "Was just the wind soundin' strange."

"Like a ghost," Brax whispered. "I heard it, too."

"Figure Cannonball's about?" Ben asked.

"Not many phantoms hereabouts," Pinto told them. "Not as I heard anyhow."

"What's that then?" Brax asked as an owl fluttered through the branches of a nearby live oak.

"Ole horned owl huntin' up a field mouse for his supper," Pinto explained.

"Ain't easy gettin' yourself growed up, is it?" Ben asked. "There's so much to learn, and no one's around to teach it."

"'Less you stay awhile," Brax added as if on cue.

The younger boys eyes turned on Pinto. Their unspoken plea bore into his heart like a rocket.

Guess there'll be no winter under the stars this year, he thought as he gazed overhead. The boys seemed to sense it, too, for they grinned and collapsed in their blankets. Only Truett stirred much that night.

Never figured him to be the one to have nightmares, Pinto thought as he roused the youngster.

"Huh?" Truett moaned.

"Havin' a bad dream," Pinto explained. "Near rolled yerself indo de fire."

Truett glanced down at the smoking tip of his blanket and sighed.

"Happened on the trail," Truett confessed. "You won't tell Ma, will you?"

"That'd be yer business," Pinto answered. "She'd be a fair one to lissen, though."

"You don't understand," Truett muttered. "I'm supposed to be the man now, and I can't even tend myself."

“I’d judge you to be doin’ passable,” Pinto argued. “Don’t try so blamed hard. Ain’t easy growin’ up at all, much less doin’ it overnight.”

“Guess not,” Truett said, softening for an instant. “Thanks for rousin’ me.”

“Wasn’t anything, Truett. You res’ easy now, hear?”

“Try my best.”

Chapter 13

By morning Truett had regained his composure, and the young man was as standoffish and hostile as ever toward Pinto. As for Ben and Brax, they'd grown weary of their elder brother's cross words and ill humor.

"Don't see what you've got to grumble about," Ben said, sizing things up. "You ride off with Jared Richardson while Brax and I chop wood and slop the hogs. Never did see anyone to complain more and do less."

"Sure didn't," Brax agreed. "And here you go railin' against Pinto when he's never done you a wrong."

Pinto rode on ahead a few hundred yards and let the three of them holler a bit. It resolved nothing, but sometimes it did some good, just blowing off steam.

As they journeyed northward, Pinto read the onrush of winter in the bronze oak and willow leaves that cascaded from bare branches. There was a bite to the wind, too. Why not? he asked himself. It was nearly November now. He'd seen snow many a time before Christmas. Of course there'd been Decembers when he and Jamie had skinned out of school and swum away the afternoon.

It was a little shy of noon when the two wagons rolled up to the Double R Ranch. Jared Richardson met them at the barn.

"So, you sold off every bushel, did you?" he asked Truett.

"Good market for corn down Fort Worth way. They got a fair number o' cattle down there waitin' fodder, too."

"Pa says the cattle market's gone south," Jared replied. "Hope it's better by the time next summer rolls around. Elsewise we'll be trailin' steers for naught."

"Well, Kansas is the place to sell beef," Truett declared. "Too many maverick longhorns in Texas. Man wants cows, he just finds himself a stretch o' open range and rounds up a few hundred of 'em."

"Ain't so many mavericks as once," Jared argued. "Good chunks o' the Llano got outfits spread across 'em now, too. Pa says more competition means a lower price. Pinto there's got the right idea. Sell horses. Always a need for 'em."

"Figure to turn de Double R to mustangs?" Pinto called.

"Pa's spoke of it," Jared confessed.

"It would make a lot of sense," Ryan Richardson insisted as he emerged from the barn with a pair of hands. The men immediately took charge of the mules and began stripping harness.

"We borrowed de critters," Pinto told the rancher. "Our job to tend 'em."

"No, I've got men to do that," Richardson argued. "I wouldn't mind a moment or two's help with something else, though."

"I figure to owe you fer de loan o' de mules and wagons," Pinto said. "You got all de time you need so far's I got it."

"Fine. Come have a look at this sorrel mare of mine. She's gone lame and I'm hanged if I can figure out why."

Pinto and Richardson marched off toward a nearby corral to examine the sorrel, leaving Jared to entertain his three young visitors. Jim and Job appeared as if by magic, and the six boys wasted no time hurrying off to look over Jared's new Winchester. When Pinto had finished working the sorrel's tendons, he turned in time to see Jared and Truett shooting tin cans off a fence rail.

"Good gun, as I hear it," Pinto said as he observed a can fly a foot in the air.

"Put a dent in a band o' rustlers easy enough," Richardson noted. "What's wrong with the mare?"

"Leg's hot," Pinto announced. "I'd judge she's pulled a tendon. I'd try some liniment. Rub it in good. Give her a res' and see, but I guess she'll recover easy enough."

"Good news. I thought it likely the trouble, but I had a horse last year with a sliver of bone split off. Thought that was only a bad tendon, too, and it wound up lamin' her. Had to put her down. This sorrel's a particular favorite o' Arabella, and I'd pay a high price to have her not disappointed."

"I'll give it a rub. Have one o' yer men work it regular. I'll come out and check on her in a day or so."

"Obliged, Lowery."

"Nothing to it."

Pinto then located a bottle of liniment in the barn and trotted over to the sorrel. As he worked on the injured tendon, he could hear the boys hooting and hollering in the distance. It was a good thing the Richardsons were wealthy. Bullets weren't cheap, and the Winchester was spitting them out quicker than lightning. It was only after he finished with the mare that he joined Richardson. The two men then walked over to where the youngsters were shooting.

"This is quite a gun, Cousin Ryan!" Truett announced. "Shoots straight and true. A repeater, too. Fifteen shots without reloadin'! A dozen men armed with these are a regular army."

"Only if they hit their target," Jared added. "You hit what, two of ten shots?"

"But I got fifteen to fire," Truett pointed out. "Even a bad shot will hit something in that many tries."

"Not if you're after deer," Jared argued. "They'd be off at the first shot. And you'd've stalked the fool buck a whole day for naught."

"The boys and I've planned a hunt," Richardson said, turning toward Truett in particular. "Last few years your pa and I fell out, Tru, but before that we scoured the Trinity bottoms for game a half-dozen times a year. Of course back then we'd likely starve if we didn't put meat on the table. Especially come winter."

"I already spoke to Tru on it, Pa," Jared explained. "Says he's of a mind to go. Wondered if maybe Ben was of an age to join us."

"And me," Brax chimed in.

"Sure, it's time you boys had a try at it," Richardson agreed. "Job and Jim've been along, carryin' gear. Brax, I'd say this year you might do the same. Rifle might be a bit much."

Braxton dropped his chin and scowled.

"There's another thing," Richardson went on to say. "Six youngsters is a trial I'm too old to face alone. We'll be needin' another man with us. I suppose Pinto might be of a mind to be persuaded to come along."

"Sure," Job said enthusiastically.

"Well, Pinto?" Ben asked.

"I thought he was off to chase range ponies," Truett said, shaking his head. "Got to be a hand or two on the Double R with a shooter's eye."

"Takes more'n an eye," Richardson declared. "Best sort of hunter's one with a nose for game and a feel for the land. I'd guess Pinto here has both."

"He ain't comin'," Truett objected. "This is a family hunt."

"Whose family?" Richardson asked. "Jared, does it trouble you to have this fellow along?"

"Not hardly," young Richardson answered. "I owe him for my chestnut mare, you know, and for more besides. He's welcome as rain in August."

"Jim? Job?"

"He tells good stories, Pa," Job said. Jim nodded his agreement.

"Ben, Brax?" the rancher asked in turn. Both encouraged Pinto to join the hunt.

"Tru, I've always known you for a generous heart," Richardson said, resting a large hand on the slim boy's shoulder. "It's up to you to come or not, but I value Pinto Lowery for a good man and I'm askin' him to come along."

"Maybe I'd best stay," Truett replied.

"You do and you'll have no buckskin britches to stave off the cold come winter," Jared grumbled. "Nor'll I abide your boasts o' fightin' rustlers up in Kansas."

"Come go with us," Ben urged. "Huh, Tru?"

"And him?" Truett asked, gazing at Pinto.

"Be a need for a steady man with a Henry," Jared answered. "Wait and see if there won't be."

"Lowery?" Richardson asked. Pinto nodded. Truett scowled, shrugged his shoulders, and surrendered.

"I figure that's eight of us," Jared told his father. "Better them deer have a lookout. Won't a one of 'em skin out on me!"

Pinto had to smile. He hadn't been any different at fifteen. As for Ben and Brax, the notion of hunting deer had those boys buzzing like a pair of addled bees. They talked of little else on the walk homeward. Only Truett was mute. The storm behind his dark eyes was another matter.

"You can't stay mad at the whole world, Truett," Elsie had scolded a few days before. "You're not the first boy to ever lose a father."

"Figure that makes it any easier?" Truett had cried.

In the two days before the Richardsons arrived to begin the hunt, it rained nearly every minute. Pinto passed most of that time in the loft, cleaning his rifle and piecing together a pair of moccasins from a cowhide. Sometimes Ben or Brax would sit and watch the work, and Winnie even sewed one side of the left moc.

"Maybe yer jus' a little gal," Pinto observed, "but you know yer business where needle and thread's concerned."

Winnie beamed and rested her head against his side. It warmed Pinto through and through.

Truett devoted those two days to breaking down the old Springfield and oiling it proper.

"You've got a gunsmith's knack with that musket," Pinto told the young man.

“Wish I had a new barrel to put on her, though,” Truett grumbled. “Jared offered to share his Winchester, but . . .”

“Seems a fair offer,” Pinto declared. “Favor’s sometimes hard to accep’, but you shouldn’t mind sharin’ a cousin’s gun.”

“Hard to think of Jared as a cousin. It’s our mas were related.”

“Then he’s a friend. Good a one as yer likely to find. Leave dis here relic fer shootin’ at raiders.”

“Ben’ll need it,” Truett pointed out.

“Ben couldn’t balance that musket with a week’s practice. I’ll help him use my Henry.”

“We ought to have a good gun in the family.”

“You got money from de cattle drive,” Pinto reminded Truett. “Bet it’s enough fer a Winchester.”

“I turned all the money over to Ma,” Truett said. “We’ll need it.”

“Bound to spare some dollars fer a rifle,” Pinto argued. “We’ll have us a ride to Decatur and see in a bit.”

“You don’t have to go. Jared’ll go along.”

“Sure. You call de tune, Truett. Bud I’m here if you need.”

Truett started to bark a reply, but he stopped himself short. For just an instant his lip trembled, and his eyes lost their anger. That didn’t last.

Ryan and Jared Richardson appeared at the Oakes farm early that next morning. It was barely light, but the skies were clear, and it promised to be a fine November day.

“We brought along a spare saddle pony for Brax,” Richardson explained as he pointed out a trim gray mare. “And a pack mule for the meat. You, Ben, and Tru have mounts.”

“We do,” Pinto said, motioning to the animals nibbling fodder in the corral. “Bes’ we saddle ’em.”

Elsie escorted her sons onto the porch. As Truett rushed to his horse, Elsie warned the younger boys to mind their elders and be careful.

"Stay close to Pinto," she urged. "He'll allow you to come to no harm."

"He said he'd let me fire off his rifle," Ben explained. "Bet I'll drop a buck big as a horse!"

"Sure, you will," Elsie said, hugging first Ben and then Braxton. She hurried over to the barn next and embraced Truett in like manner. Finally she turned to Pinto.

"No need to say it," he told her. "I'll keep 'em from harm, ma'am."

Elsie returned to the house, and Pinto climbed atop the white-faced stallion. Ben rode over on old Sugarcane and led the way to the others. Then the eight of them trotted off toward the Trinity bottoms.

It wasn't a hunt in the fashion Pinto was accustomed. Deer were thick as fleas along that stretch of the river, and sign was everywhere.

"Bet there's not a berry bush or sapling for ten miles that's not gnawed to a stub," Jared said as he pointed to several clear tracks in the sandy soil. "Look, there's one now."

Pinto followed the fifteen-year-old's long arm toward the river. A whitetail bounded along the bank and vanished into a nearby thicket.

"Leave the horses here," Richardson instructed. "We'll go ahead on foot. Tie 'em off with a double loop, boys. I don't plan to carry my weight in venison back to the ranch nor to feed every wolf pack for twenty miles, either."

"Best you and me follow Pa and Job," Jared told Truett. "Jim's sure to tag along last. Your brothers can stick to Pinto like your ma said."

"They should be with me," Truett argued.

"Can't but two of us shoot this one rifle," Jared said, shaking his head. "Bring Brax along if you want. He ain't shootin'. If Ben wants a try, he'd best share the Henry."

"Ben?" Truett asked.

"Go ahead on," Ben answered.

"Brax?" Truett said, turning to his younger brother.

"Ma said stick with Pinto," Brax said, sliding an inch nearer the mustanger. "'Sides, I'd only be in your way."

"I'll look after 'em," Pinto vowed.

"You ain't our pa, you know," Truett remarked bitterly. "Ain't your place to—"

"Figure it's yers, Truett?" Pinto asked. "I'll turn de Henry over to you and let you take charge."

"Tru?" Jared asked.

"I never shot a Henry rifle once in my whole life," Truett confessed. "How'm I to show 'em to do somethin' I don't know myself?"

"Now there's wisdom speakin'," Pinto declared. "It's all I been tryin' do tell you all along. Never said I'd walk in anybody's boots but my own. Not yer pa's nor yers. But give yerself some time, Tru."

"We huntin' or gabbin'?" Richardson called from the river.

"Huntin', Pa," Jared said, waving Tru to his side.

They walked a quarter of a mile or so before reaching a muddy stretch of bank. Deer tracks led from dense underbrush to the river, and Ryan Richardson spaced out his companions along a knoll overlooking the deer run. The wind blew sharply out of the north and stung their eyes, but it would carry no alarming scent to the deer approaching the river. Theirs was the perfect blind.

The first buck appeared half an hour after Pinto nestled himself among the scrub oaks and buffalo grass. Richardson motioned to leave the animal be, and soon three does joined the big buck. Others followed until there were close to a dozen animals enjoying their afternoon drink.

Richardson silently pointed to himself and raised one finger. In like fashion he bid Jared take the second shot and Pinto the third. Afterward it wouldn't matter as the alerted deer would scatter in every direction.

Pinto readied his rifle, but he didn't elect to take the first shot. Instead he motioned Ben over. The boy lay at Pinto's side, eagerly reaching for the rifle. Pinto cradled it in Ben's long, thin arms and helped him to sight down the barrel.

"Hold her steady, and aim fer de ches'," Pinto whispered. Ben took a deep breath and slowly exhaled. He took another and fired a split second after Ryan Richardson dropped a big buck on the left. Ben's bullet struck a second buck in the neck, dropping the animal to the ground. Jared's shot hit a smallish doe.

"Your turn, Pinto," an excited Ben said as he gave up the Henry. Pinto calmly advanced a second cartridge into the firing chamber and drew down on the fleeing deer. He picked out a doe and fired, dropping the animal a foot shy of the river.

"Can I?" Brax pleaded.

"Second shot?" Ben asked.

"We got food enough," Pinto asserted. "And work enough skinnin' and butcherin'."

"Yes, sir," Ben muttered. He then perked up and started down the hillside.

"Not yet!" Pinto shouted as he yanked Ben back into cover. "Jus' 'cause we done our shootin' don't mean everybody has."

Sure enough two shots rang out from the left a moment later, and Ben shuddered. Neither bullet found a deer.

"All clear here!" Pinto called.

"Clear here!" Job countered. The eight hunters then emerged from their cover and began collecting their kills. Jared's doe required a second shot, and his father's buck had somehow dragged itself fifty feet or so into the woods.

"Look here, Tru!" Ben exclaimed as he dashed down beside his buck. "Where's yours?"

"Halfway to tomorrow, little brother," Tru said, shaking his head. "Moved a hair before I fired. A clean miss."

"We got four," Brax announced. "That's enough."

"Not if we're all to have a new coat," Truett muttered.

"Tru, you can have my deer's hide," Jared offered. "Only fair. Was my shot scattered 'em. Pa and I come for the meat and the adventure. I'm no hand at tannin' hides."

"Pinto is," Brax boasted. "Look at his new mocs."

"Was yer little sister mos'ly sewed 'em up," Pinto told the Oakes youngsters. "As fer tannin' buckskin, ain't any secrets to it."

"You'll teach us then?" Ben asked.

"Us, too?" Job added.

"Anybody cares to learn," Pinto promised.

Chapter 14

For a week the Oakes family feasted on venison steaks. What wasn't eaten fresh was salted away against later need. As Pinto stripped the tough deerhides of dried flesh and soaked them in oak bark to toughen the texture, he felt winter's approach. Nightly the north wind shrieked across the land, and frost now greeted each dawn. By now birds had set off southward, and all but the live oaks down by the river had shed their leaves.

"It's grown cold," Elsie noted as she built up the fire one night after supper. "That barn must be an ice house."

"I'm pretty far off de ground, and dere's plenty o' hay," Pinto explained. "Could be warmer, I'd warrant, but it'll get colder 'fore it brightens much. I got blankets, you know."

"I know you're killin' yourself to work those deerhides into jackets and trousers for the boys. And you don't have anything resembling a proper winter coat for yourself."

"Intended de pick up a buff hide and shape it fer a coat. Forgot. Been occupied with things."

"Well, you'll do no one any good frozen," she complained. "I've got one of Tully's old coats put back. I cut down the other so Tru could wear it."

"He won't favor me wearin' his pa's coat," Pinto argued.

"I'll speak with him first," Elsie promised. "You know, it's a puzzlement how Truett's actin'. He told me yesterday he's the only one misses his pa. Me, I think of Tully every wakin' minute. Shouldn't I? We'd known each other since we were walkin'. But Tru never got on with Tully."

"Jared Richardson said that."

"And now, to take on so, you'd judge they were twin branches off the same tree."

"Could be they come to terms on de trail north."

"Maybe, but Ryan told me different. Tully gave Tru a whippin' the mornin' his horse threw him."

"Well, that's not so hard to unnerstand then. Boy didn't measure up. Who can say? Maybe Tru hoped somethin'd happen. Now he's gone and gotten guilty. Makes sense of a kind."

"I suppose it does," Elsie agreed. "Never looked at it from that direction. I need to do some talkin' to him."

"Be careful you don't give him to feel he ain't needed," Pinto warned. "Promised Tully he'd see to things. Been hard doin' that, but he's tried. Give him to know you lean on him."

"How is it, Pinto Lowery, you know so much? I thought you spent your life around horses."

"Boy critter's not so different from a spry colt," Pinto said, grinning. "Jus' use a different liniment fer mendin' 'em, and you can pass up de bit mos' times."

She laughed at the remark, and he did, too. Then she threw a fresh log on the fire, and Pinto set off for the barn to resume his work on the hides.

That night the wind whined eerily, and the barn itself seemed to shudder under its force. Pinto was twice awakened by the nervous stomping of the horses out in the corral, and he finally wrapped himself in a blanket and pulled on his trousers. Half asleep, he didn't think to step into his boots, so his nigh frozen feet managed to collect a dozen or so splinters from the loft ladder and then numb themselves on the walk over to the corral.

"Easy, critters," Pinto called as he opened the gate and guided the horses toward the barn. In short order he nudged them into stalls and returned, shivering, to the loft.

The sound of the horses down below was comforting. Before, with just the shrill wind to torment him, Pinto had been particularly downcast. Now he had company of the best kind.

He dreamed that night of sleek horses and yellow-haired girls. There were no musket balls or cannonades, nor even fierce winds to haunt him. The dream took him far away and left him oddly warm and renewed when dawn showered the barn with golden light next morning.

"That's a dream I could've had a hair longer," he mumbled as he struggled into his clothes. The air hung heavy, and the draft creeping through the gaps between the planks tinged it with an icy touch. The horses felt it, too, and they stomped fitfully.

"Storm's brewin'," Pinto announced when he joined the others for breakfast. "Bes' get ourselves ready for it."

"There's hardly a cloud in the sky," Truett objected. "A little cold, maybe, but it's nearly winter, after all."

"May not be clouds yet, but dey'll come along by and by. Mark that fer a fac'."

"I feel it, too," Elsie declared. "We'll get the shutters up and put by an extra stock of wood. Water, too."

"Northers hit quick, too," Pinto said, turning to the children. "Winnie, no runnin' down to de creek, hear? You boys keep close by, too. Powerful mean these storms. Freeze a full-grown man solid. Boys, well, hate to think on it."

"You heard him, Braxton, Benjamin, Truett? Stay within hollerin' distance of the house today."

"Yes, Ma," the three of them agreed.

"Now let's get my eggs eaten 'fore they're cold as that wind out there," Elsie said, grinning.

"Maybe we can build a snow critter if we get enough powder," Brax suggested.

"I don't expect we'll have a blizzard," Elsie replied. But the look in Pinto's eyes betrayed his fears, and she lost her smile. Thereafter Pinto gobbled down his food only a hair faster than the others did. While Winnie helped her mother clear away the plates, Pinto and Brax started in on the shutters.

"You chop stove wood," Pinto told Ben. "Truett, maybe you'd have a try at fillin' that spare water barrel."

"Done in no time," Truett replied. Ben grabbed an ax and started for the two cottonwoods Pinto had dragged in from the river bottoms the day before. Cottonwoods weren't much of a staying tree, but they did grow big. There was plenty of wood on them, even if they had a bad habit of burning quick and not so hot as oak.

Amid the cracking of the ax and the hammering of shutters, the wind was but a distant whine. Even so, it drove icy daggers into Pinto's exposed hands and face. Little Brax shivered, and his mouth blew fog puffs everytime he breathed.

"Bes' get along inside," Pinto finally ordered when he spied the blue tint of Brax's fingers. "Get yerself alongside that fire and warm up."

"Shutters aren't all up," Brax argued.

"Ben'll be along to help," Pinto replied, pulling the freezing ten-year-old close and rubbing warmth back into his frail body. Pinto then ushered Brax inside the house. Elsie took one look at her youngest boy's wan face and took charge.

"Need a hand?" Ben called from the woodpile. He had a good wool coat and sheepskin gloves, so the cold had less of a bite. Pinto nodded, and Ben drove the bit of his ax into the chopping stump and headed over. The two of them hurriedly affixed the remaining shutters and then dashed inside to warm themselves.

"Brrrr," Ben said as he kicked off his ice-coated boots.

Brax helped Pinto over to the hearth and pried a frozen blanket from his shoulders.

"That settles one matter," Elsie said, rummaging around in a trunk until she produced a worn woolen coat. "You'll have this on next time you step outside this house."

"Pa's coat," Ben mumbled. "You saved it."

"When did Ma ever let loose of somethin' what could be used?" Brax asked, laughing as he started rubbing Pinto's feet.

"Be too big," Winnie judged. "Pinto's littler'n Pa, except for in the hands."

"Feet, too," Brax added. "Pa ran to small in the foot. Me too."

"You run to small in everything, Brax," Ben noted. "I've seen chickens with more skin over their bones."

"You ain't plannin' to eat me, are you?" Brax asked. "If I was lazy and did no more work'n you did, I'd be plump as Mary Johnson."

"Who?" Elsie asked.

"Girl that tends the mercantile counter in Defiance now," Ben explained. "Must weigh three hundred pounds. I heard she come from a circus."

"That's unkind, Benjamin," Elsie scolded. "Winnie, pour off some hot water in a basin so your brothers can wash up for dinner. Braxton, come help set table. Where's Tru gotten to anyway?"

"Went off to look over the stock," Ben explained.

"He what?" Pinto gasped. "Not out in that?"

Even though the windows were shuttered and the door bolted, they all knew what was outside. For several minutes delicate flakes of snow had blown under the door. The norther had arrived. Wise County was becoming a world of ice and snow.

"When did he go, Ben?" Elsie asked, trying to remain calm.

"After fillin' the water barrels," Ben answered. "Hour ago. Maybe two."

"He wouldn't have stayed out in the open," Elsie argued. "Like as not he's gone over to the RR with Jared. The two of them are forever up to something."

"Sure," Pinto said, inwardly unconvinced. "Young fool. I warned him, remember?"

"Yeah, but Tru ain't much on advice takin'," Ben observed. "If you was to say the sun rises in the mornin', he'd tell you it comes up at midnight."

"He's nowhere near that bad," Elsie insisted. "But he's bound to feel a switch this time. I won't have him kill himself short of his fifteenth birthday."

She was near crying, Pinto saw, and she might have broken down had not Ben given her a needed hug. She then announced dinner ready. Pinto followed Brax over to the wash basin. After cleaning up, he bowed his head while Elsie said a brief prayer.

"And Lord, give a look after Truett. He's rash and more foolish than not, but we love him. He's a good boy who deserves another chance."

She ladled out portions of venison stew then, and Pinto lapped his up hungrily. In spite of the shared concern over Truett, the cold had seemingly hollowed out their stomachs. There wasn't a hint of anything remaining when they finished.

"Poor Tru," Brax said, wiping his mouth with a napkin. "Missin' a good dinner's worse'n a switchin'."

"I believe he's right, ma'am," Pinto agreed. "Warmed me up proper. Maybe I'll step out and have a look at de animals now."

"Take the coat," Elsie instructed. "Ben, see if you can fish out those gloves, too."

"Tru took 'em, Ma," Ben explained.

"Then at least his hands're warm," Elsie remarked. "Pinto, you have your look, but don't linger."

"I won't," Pinto promised.

He made, in truth, only the briefest of inspections. The big black and the packhorse were both accustomed to rough life, and the cold was survivable in the barn. The mottled gelding that had served Tru on the long ride to Kansas and old Sugarcane should have done as well, but the poor horse snorted and stomped. Yes, that pony felt the cold.

At that instant a strange foreboding came over Pinto. He turned away and started toward the house. Snow was beginning to fall by the bucketfuls, and already drifts half a foot high piled up against the northern wall of the house. Through a white mist trotted a horse.

"Tru's back!" Ben yelled, rushing out to meet the horse. It wasn't until Ben led the animal to the barn that Pinto saw the truth. Truett Oakes was nowhere to be found. His horse had come in alone.

"No!" Elsie cried when Pinto explained it to her half an hour later in the house. "Not Truett, too! First Tully. Now Tru!"

"He's tough, Ma," Ben argued. "Holed up someplace. Maybe at the RR."

"No, he's hurt . . . and alone," Elsie cried. "I feel it. With this snow he'll freeze sure."

"No, he's got a good coat and warm gloves," Pinto reminded her. "Probably he's found cover. Tied off the horse, but it bein' a smart critter, horse took off fer home."

"Do you really believe he's all right?" Elsie asked.

"Don't see much anything else to think."

And yet Truett didn't return. The storm slackened for a time, and Pinto expected the fourteen-year-old to appear, a trifle shaky and very cold. But Truett remained unaccounted for, and the storm threatened to worsen.

"What'll we do?" Elsie asked after a bit.

"Nothin' else we can do," Pinto muttered. "I'm goin' to find him."

"No," Elsie argued. "You don't have a clue as to where he went, and . . ."

"I'll find him," Pinto assured her. "I got a horse bred on hardship. And a hide tuff as steel."

"Be careful," Elsie urged.

"Ain't fer a careful man to do," Pinto confessed. "Don't you fret, though. I'll find him."

By the time Pinto had pulled on two extra shirts and Elsie had wrapped his hands in shreds of an old shawl, the snow was coming down in earnest. Worse, the shining surface was iced over and treacherous. Pinto slipped three times on his way to the barn.

Fool's errand, he told himself. But one way or another he was bound to locate Truett Oakes.

He got the black saddled and ready, but once out in the white nightmare, the mustang turned skittish.

"I know, boy," Pinto whispered as he managed to climb onto the big horse's back. "Wouldn't wish dis storm on a Yankee, but there's a boy we got to find."

And with that said, Pinto gave the animal a light kick. Now the flurries danced in eerie spirals as the wind caught them on their way down. Tracking was nigh impossible. A print left two minutes before was quickly filled with new snow. It was as if an ivory blanket had been draped across the land.

Pinto headed for the creek. That's where they'd piled fodder for the cattle, and if Truett had gone to look after the stock, perhaps he'd ridden that way. Then, too, the RR Ranch lay that way. There was the odd chance the boy had set off to locate Jared Richardson.

Pinto made his way through the drifting snow, searching to the right and then the left. It was a world painted in white mists, though, and even the stark outlines of the trees were now blurred with snow and ice. Whole branches shattered as their ice-filled hollows expanded. The creek bottom sounded like a battlefield.

He was thirty yards short of the north ford when he spied a dark blotch just shy of the woods. Another man, one less frozen or desperate, would have glanced past it. Pinto turned the black and struggled against the drifts. He reached down and snatched the half-buried object from the snow.

It was Truett's brushed leather hat, the one he was so proud of. Likely the boy'd paid too much for it in some Wichita store, but Pinto recalled the swagger that pride put in a young man's walk when he donned his first real hat.

Won't be far, Pinto realized. Truett wouldn't leave that hat behind. Not if he still had his senses, that is.

Pinto rested the hat on his saddlehorn and rolled off the saddle. He took care to tie the reins to a willow limb lest the black turn sensible and head homeward. He struggled on ahead through the piled snow, snagging his trousers on hidden briers and gashing his chin on the wicked thorns of a black locust limb. As he reached the shelter of the trees, he bellowed out again and again.

"Truett! Tru! Where've you gotten to, boy?"

Over and over Pinto called, but there was no response. Finally, near a rocky outcropping, Pinto detected a moan. There was a hint of movement, too, and he hurried in that direction.

"Lord, you've gone and froze yerself," Pinto gasped. Truett's dark hair was glazed, and his lower half was buried by a snowdrift. He struggled to move, but his lips were blue and coated with ice. His chest barely moved as he fought to breathe.

"Don't you worry yerself," Pinto said as he broke the boy loose from his ice tomb. Shards of ice cracked and splintered, but Pinto freed the young man nevertheless. The boy's legs stirred to life, and Pinto managed to shake a word out of Truett amid a convulsive cough.

"Ma?" Truett whimpered.

"Waitin' fer you with a switch," Pinto said as he rubbed life into the youngster's arms. "Fine notion, coverin' up with snow. Good's a blanket."

"I . . . got . . . lost," Truett managed.

"Fool to go ridin' with a world o' snow comin'," Pinto scolded. "Maybe nex' time you'll have ears for a warnin'. But bein' young, I don't figure to bet money on it. Can't get tall without doin' a fool thing or two."

Truett didn't try to respond. A hint of color was returning to his face, though, and as Pinto wiped ice and snow from cheeks and eyebrows, life revisited the boy's eyes.

"I, uh, I . . ."

"You save dem words fer later," Pinto suggested as he bent down and draped Truett over one shoulder. "Got a horse waitin' to get us home. Now you jus' shake some life back into you while I do some walkin'."

Pinto sagged under the weight at first, but after a few steps Truett seemed no more than a sack of oats. Oh, it was a squirming worm of a sack, to be sure, but what had seemed solid and substantial under his father's heavy coat now revealed itself as illusion.

Pinto stumbled through the tangled underbrush to the big black, then managed to help Truett up behind the saddle. Pinto himself untied the reins and mounted with a shudder.

"Hold on good as you can," Pinto said as he helped Truett wrap near frozen arms around the waist of his rescuer. "Got no time to fish you out o' de snow."

The stallion then turned and rushed through the heavy snows. The horse sensed Pinto's urgency, or perhaps just felt the cold as its riders did. Whether it was the one thing or the other, the mustang managed to halve its outbound time.

Back at the farm, Pinto pulled the horse to a halt. Elsie raced out to take charge of Truett, and Ben grabbed the horse's reins.

"Get inside," Ben ordered, pointing Pinto toward the door. "I'll get the black into the barn."

"Give him a good rub," Pinto urged. "Some witch hazel'd help. And . . ."

"I know what to do," Ben answered as he set off with the horse. "You don't want to cough out the winter, better get on inside."

"Yessir," Pinto replied with a grin. He then stumbled to the door and fell inside the house.

Chapter 15

Pinto drifted in and out of a vague sort of consciousness those next three hours. He recalled eager hands leading him to the fire, peeling off his frozen clothes, and rubbing new life into his numb hands and feet. There was a mug of hot broth, too, and little Winnie's grinning face asking him if he didn't feel better now he was warmed up.

It was all a blur. When his eyes finally came into focus and his head cleared, he was lying between two thick quilts alongside a roaring fire.

"Better?" Ben asked, leaning over and placing a hand on Pinto's chest. "Fever's broke at least. Scared us, you know, fallin' down like you did. Ma thought you rescued Tru only to kill yourself in the bargain. Never saw her so stirred up in my life. She didn't even yell that much when Pa died!"

"Truett?" Pinto asked.

"Oh, he's soakin' in a tub. Brax's watchin' him. Wouldn't let Ma near him, sayin' he was grown now and it wasn't proper. Who's he think cut off his shirt and thawed him out, I wonder."

"I thank you fer seein' after my horse, Ben."

"Wasn't so much, seein' you saved me a brother. I don't know who was happier gettin' home, you, Tru, or that stallion."

"Close race, eh?

"You know it's gotten worse out there, too. Snow's seven, eight inches deep. Ma said you figured a blizzard. Weren't far wrong this time."

"No, but I wish I had been."

Pinto then took a deep breath and sat up. His hands were wrapped in cotton strips, and he started to peel them.

"Don't, Pinto. Ma's scared of frostbite," Ben said, shaking his head. "I figured your toes to be in trouble, too, but a little warm water brought back their color just fine."

Pinto drew back the quilt and had a look. His legs were swallowed by a pair of Tully Oakes's old overalls. His bare feet were a trifle paler than normal, but Pinto moved his toes just fine.

"An old soldier trick," Pinto told Ben. "Had more'n our share o' frosbit feet. Had one poor fellow to lose three toes."

"Feelin' up to some supper? Ma put a platter of venison sausage on the sideboard, and she's keepin' a pot of coffee hot on the stove. I could slice some bread and make you up somethin'."

"In a bit," Pinto said, nodding in thanks. "Jus' now I'd rather walk a hair."

"Can walk more'n that if you want," Ben said, laughing. "Your whole self if you want."

"Figure I can, do you?"

"Just as long as it's inside. Wind's howlin' somethin' fierce outside."

"Where's yer ma gone do?"

"Worked awful hard gettin' you and Tru thawed," Ben explained. "She and Winnie went and took a nap in the back room."

"Ain't it cold in dere, Ben?"

"They got a fireplace in there, Pinto. I lit the fire myself. It's warm enough. Want some of that coffee?"

"Sure," Pinto agreed, rising to his feet. He followed Ben into the kitchen, then stepped back.

"Didn't mean to bother you," Pinto apologized when he saw Truett. The elder Oakes boy was standing beside an empty tub, pulling on a pair of oversized trousers over flannel drawers. A wool blanket was draped over his bare shoulders, and his hair resembled a bundle of raw cotton dyed walnut brown.

"Don't figure you need say sorry for anything this day," Truett replied as he buttoned his trousers. "To me, especially. Ma told me all you did. I can't remember much past seein' your face come out of the snow."

"Mus've scared you out of a year's growin'," Pinto said, laughing.

"Looked good as gold to me just then. Ben, figure you can take Brax off someplace a minute or so. I got somethin' to tell Mr. Lowery."

"Sure," Ben agreed, waving Braxton along. The two straw-haired boys vanished into the front room. For a moment Truett busied himself rubbing the moisture out of his skin. Standing there, bare to the waist, the boy appeared younger than before. It was a brave show he put on, Pinto decided.

"Sometimes words can be hard to come by," Truett said, swallowing hard.

"Don't need words mos' o' de time. Don't now. I guess I know what's in yer head."

"I got to say it."

"Sure, I see. Go ahead on."

"I been hard on you. Unkind hard on you."

"A hair maybe," Pinto admitted.

"Ben and Brax laid into me on it more'n once, but they didn't understand. Pa's gone, and it ain't right you come and take his place."

"Never tried to do that, Truett."

"Maybe not, but you're doin' it just the same. I promised Pa to look after things, but it's you does that. Till today I thought I could manage. Now I see I was wrong . . . near dead wrong. I'm sorry for what I said in the past. We do need you here. Pa was right. I'm just a stumblefoot boy no matter how hard I try to be somethin' else."

"I don't figure you've done so bad," Pinto argued.

"You needn't lie. I hear others talk. For a time I thought it was only Pa. He never took a shine to me, you see, nor to the things I did," Truett explained. "I watch Jared and his pa, and I wonder what I could've done so wrong that Pa wouldn't like me. I worked hard, hard as anybody I ever knew. On the way to Kansas, I kept to my saddle longer'n anybody, even though I was near the youngest. I'd've showed him he had a son to be proud of if only that horse hadn't thrown him. He should've been ridin' my horse that day. His was weary, and I . . ."

"He ask fer yer horse?" Pinto interrupted.

"No, but I should've . . ."

"Can't be forever wonderin' this or that," Pinto advised. "I los' my own pa, and was a thing on earth I could do 'bout it. Life don't always turn as you'd have it, but things sort 'emselves out in de end."

"Most times you sound like you know," Truett said, managing half a grin. "It's awful hard sometimes knowin' what to do when you're just fourteen."

"Addin' years don't make it easier," Pinto said, laughing to himself. "I done plenty of fool things in my time, and more'n a few been since I was full grown."

"That's not much comfort, you know. Anyway, I did want to thank you for draggin' me in from the snow. I'd be dead if you'd left me. It weighs heavy on me knowin' I wouldn't've gone after you if your horse'd ridden in."

"Seems to me you let yer Pa's passin' burden you enough already," Pinto said, stepping over beside the young man. "You know, I passed half a year in de Petersburg trenches, holdin' out agains' dem Yankees. Was a fair share o' fightin' early on, but by and by it settled down. We had Carolina tobacco that winter, and de Yanks sniffed it and hollered over dey'd swap us coffee fer some. Pretty soon we had ourselves a brisk trade goin'. Made ourselves a sort o' truce."

"How'd you do that?" Truett asked.

"Put grudges behind us and shook hands," Pinto answered, offering up his own hand in friendship. Truett clasped it with his damp fingers, and the truce was sealed.

"Ma said some time back she'd favor you stayin' through winter," Truett explained as he dressed himself. "Wanted me to ask you. How'd you feel 'bout that? I know you had your heart set on running down some range ponies."

"Winter's no time to ride the Llano alone," Pinto replied. "I'd be obliged for the shelter."

"You'd earn it. As you have been. Understand, you'll get a healthy portion of pesterin' from Ben and Brax, not to mention Winnie."

"Havin' company close can be a comfort, though. Thing I got to know's how you stand on me."

"I don't know how to answer you, Mr. Lowery."

"Ain't no mister to me. Jus' Pinto."

"I don't find trustin' anybody very easy," Truett confessed.

"Sure, it's hard mos'ly. But I'm a man to know ridin' alone's no tonic. Dries a man's insides."

"Yeah, I been feelin' hollow ever since Pa fell. Maybe even before."

"Well, you lean on ole Pinto if you need. And once de sky clears some, you find some mischief to get indo. Maybe with ole Jared."

"Sounds just fine to me," Truett said, brightening.

"By and by de hurt passes, you see. And times get better."

"I hope so," Truett said, sighing. "I truly do."

An hour or so later, after taking a turn at the warming tub himself, Pinto mustered the nerve to have a look outside. The wind had eased, but the ground was buried by a foot of glazed snow. The gray plank walls of the barn were painted an eerie white, and long icicles dangled from the eaves. Standing alone on the porch, even wrapped in three blankets, the damp and cold near froze him stiff.

"Get back inside here!" Elsie scolded as she cracked open the door. "Now."

"Time I got back to de barn," he explained.

"You can't mean to go there," she insisted, reaching over and clamping a firm hand on his arm. She dragged him back inside and slammed the door shut on the icy air.

"She's right," Truett said from beside the hearth. "It's too cold in the barn, what with no fire and all. We don't even use our room around the side when it snows. Stay here by the fire, with us."

"All my gear . . ." Pinto began.

"Oh, that," Ben said, grinning. "I fetched it along when I put your horse in his stall. Wasn't all that much, and we got plenty o' warmer beddin'."

"Clothes need patchin', too," Winnie announced. "Me and Ma'll start on 'em tomorrow."

"Some'd be best used for rags," Elsie added. "Next trip to town you spend some of that money you've put away to outfit yourself proper. If you're goin' to stay under my roof, I'll expect you to be presentable."

"Elsie, I'd . . ."

"We decided, the five of us," Truett explained, wrapping an arm around his mother. "Once it warms up, if you want to go back to your solitude, then you go. Just now you need the fire."

"Wouldn't have been any solitude anyhow," Ben declared. "We climbed up there most nights and half the mornin's."

"You'll have to get used to some snorin'," Pinto warned.

"Can't be as bad as Pa," Winnie said, giggling.

"Naw, he's not half so bad," Brax said, adding a log to the fire. "We heard him comin' home from Ft. Worth. Shoot, Tru can snore good's Pinto."

The youngsters ushered him over to the fire and huddled in a half circle around the dancing flames. Elsie was there, too, on the far side with Winnie. He saw her eyes gaze his way, with warmth and rare tenderness. Little Brax burrowed his head under Pinto's right arm, too, and the closeness was near overpowering.

"You all right, Pinto?" Ben asked as the color seemed to flow from the mustanger's face.

"Jus' fine," Pinto insisted. "Ain't so used to company's all."

"You'll get used to it," Elsie assured him. "Can be tight quarters in this house come winter."

Yes, Pinto told himself. And that would make riding off come spring all the harder. A year ago Pinto might have vowed to leave the first chance the weather provided. But he ached for company just then, and no amount of sensible figuring would prompt him to turn his back on the sense of belonging he felt that moment. No, the Llano never welcomed a lone man come winter. Nor any other time.

Pinto Lowery knew only too well.

Chapter 16

Winter hit northern Texas hard that year. It took half a week for that first snow to melt, and twice before Christmas other blizzards tormented the farms and ranches of Wise County. Whenever a hint of sun appeared, Pinto rode out with Truett to have a look after the stock. Sometimes they would drag fodder to a small herd of cattle. Other times they would drive animals out to fresh water and grass.

On other days Pinto would shoulder his Henry and lead the Oakes boys on a hunt. Once or twice they dropped a deer, but most of the time the hunters settled for rabbits or squirrels. Once the real cold settled in, game became scarce. As meat supplies dwindled, Truett would cut out a steer for butchering.

Aside from putting meat on the table, there were hides for working. Pinto already had Truett working on a pair of buckskin trousers. Ben and Brax had been wearing shirts of deerhide since mid-November. With Christmas growing near, Pinto held back some of the hides and worked secretly some afternoons in the loft. By Christmas Eve he'd sewn a warm pair of rabbit fur gloves for Elsie and a second pair for Winnie. Two coons treed in the Trinity bottoms had yielded skin caps for Ben and Brax. Finally Pinto had crafted a fine pair of saddlebags for Truett out of cowhide.

Be some kind o' surprise come Chris'mas mornin', Pinto thought. Only days before, Elsie had warned there was little cash for frills. Looking around the dinner table, Pinto had judged the words not needed. Even Winnie had taken note of the dwindling contents of the sugar bowl, and Pinto had provided a fresh tin of coffee himself, along with a shiny new Winchester rifle he decided couldn't wait for a holiday.

"Good huntin' gun's sure do earn its price back," Pinto explained when he replaced the ancient Springfield with the new rifle.

"We ought to pay for it, Ma," Truett had argued. "If we're goin' to be the ones use it."

"Certainly," Elsie had agreed. "And Pinto ought to have wages."

She fetched her purse and doled out the rifle's cost together with fifty dollars' wages. Later, in private, Pinto returned the money.

"Better to spend it on new shoes for de little ones. I'll take what's owed me in stock come spring roundup," he told her. "Cash's scarce, I'd judge, and needed."

"It doesn't mean you aren't due a fair wage," she'd argued.

"Different sorts o' pay, Elsie," he had replied. "Warm fire and good company's one."

"Then we owe you double, Pinto. And more."

Come Christmas Eve, everyone living within twenty miles of the RR was invited over for a bit of celebrating. A Methodist circuit preacher would read some verse, and Ryan Richardson would provide a yearling calf for the spit. Fiddlers would offer up music, and those who chose could dance or sing or gossip away half the day.

Jared arrived a little shy of midday with a wagon, and the Oakeses piled in the bed. Pinto and Tru sat up front with young Richardson. As the mules started south toward the Double R, Ben drew out his mouth organ and fetched up a tune. Amid the singing and good feeling, Pinto hardly felt the bite of a bitter December wind.

Once at the Richardson place, the boys dashed off to find some mischief. Winnie quickly located a handful of farmgirls intent on emptying a platter of sugar cakes, and Elsie found herself drawn off by a band of clucking females.

"You seem to've lost a family," J. B. Dotham observed as he wandered over. "Christmas meetin's always the same. I barely seen my own boys; and the hands, well, one hint of petticoat and they run off like stampedin' bulls."

"Yeah, I chased a sniff o' lilac water or two in my time," Pinto added, laughing.

"And now?"

"Well, I'll admit to havin' a glance 'round."

"If you won't tell Amanda, my wife, I'll confess I took a look or two myself."

"Comanches couldn't pry it out o' me," Pinto swore.

"I looked over the Oakes youngsters, too. A little threadbare this year."

"Times been hard, what wid their Pa dead and all."

"Times were just as hard when he wasn't. New pair of trousers and a fresh shirt would be nice, but I judge they've all of them filled out some since summer's end. Unusual for farmers. Most years winter takes a toll. You done some fine work over there, I'd guess."

"Oh, was mos'ly Elsie."

"Was it? Not to hear Jared talk. By his accounts you must be the best rifle shot and the hardest rider in all Texas."

"Boys stretch de truth as a rule," Pinto declared, shaking his head. "I confess I've dropped more deer dis year'n I have since '67. Too many of 'em in de bottomland anyhow. Food's been welcome, and de hides, too."

"I noticed the buckskins."

"No swap-off fer cotton come summer, but dey warm a body in de winter."

Elsie moved past them then, surrounded by a flock of women. She barely managed a hello to Dotham and a nod to Pinto before they hurried her along.

"Elsie's durned popular," Pinto observed.

"Strange how bothered everybody's come to be about her,"

Dotham added. "When Tully was around, nobody wasted a worry on her, and he was about as much use to her as a hammer is to a flea."

"What do you figure's changed things?" Pinto asked.

"You," Dotham said, frowning. "It's a small world out here, you know. Jared says something, and Arabella picks it up. Next thing you know it's racin' around Defiance and halfway to Austin."

"Jus' what is it racin' 'round, Mr. Dotham?"

"Word has it you've moved into the house."

"Have," Pinto said, grinding his teeth. "Was firs' snow, and de wind near froze anything that moved. Tru got himself los', and I fetched him home."

"I heard the tale, and I merit it was a fine, brave thing for a hired man to risk his neck over a fool fourteen-year-old."

"Been a man or two put 'emselves out fer me when I wasn't much older," Pinto explained. "Never should've allowed 'em to talk me into beddin' in de house. Wouldn't've if I guessed it's bring on harm."

"It hasn't," Dotham argued. "Most people hereabouts would hold it against a farmer to leave a man to freeze in his barn come winter. But where a widow's concerned . . ."

"Rules's different, eh? Well, cold or no, I'll go back to that lof'. Appreciate yer speakin' do me on it."

"It's as a friend, you know. Of Elsie's as well as yours. I don't grudge the either of you a touch of comfort, but . . ."

"Ain't any comfortin' gone on," Pinto said forcefully. "Anybody sayin' there has been's de worse kind o' liar."

"I take your word on that, though I personally believe the both of you would profit from each other's company. Been a time since we had a weddin' hereabouts. Those boys need a man to look up to, and I wager they've found one. Elsie needs a man, and little Winnie dotes on you. Everybody sees that."

"I figure everybody's gone and put a nose in business ain't their own," Pinto responded angrily.

"If I have, excuse it for concern. But take a moment to ponder the possibilities, too. You wouldn't have stayed if you felt nothing, and it would be a fine base for a horse breeder. This county's always short of saddle ponies."

"That'll be yer lookout come spring," Pinto warned. "I'll be out on de Llano by then."

He passed the remainder of the afternoon in rare ill humor. He sat with the family at the Bible reading, but otherwise found other business to occupy himself.

"Come join the dancin'," Elsie urged a bit later. "I'm shy a partner, you know."

"Ain't got de heart fer it," Pinto answered. "Maybe Tru'll turn you 'round de floor."

"Tru's got Emily Blasingame to entertain him," she explained.

"Then I'd bet Richardson's at loose ends."

"I suppose it's a woman's curse to love dancin' and find herself at the mercy of sour men. Well, you go ahead and enjoy your solitude, Pinto Lowery! I'm goin' to dance if I have to ask Grandpa Jones to lead me out!"

It was well past dusk when Jared drove them back to the Oakes place. Ben and Brax were jabbering away about the food, and Winnie hummed the melody of a dance tune. Truett and Jared spoke of hunting deer that next week. Pinto sat on the hard wooden bench seat and tried to steel himself against the cold.

Once at the house, the children hurried out of the wagonbed and sped to the door. Pinto helped Elsie carry along two baskets of food Arabella Richardson insisted on sending while Truett took a moment to thank Jared for the wagon ride.

"Merry Christmas!" Jared called as he stirred the mules into motion.

"Merry Christmas!" the Oakeses replied.

"Now it's off to bed with you little ones," Elsie said, ushering them inside. "Tru, stoke us a fire, won't you?"

"I'll fetch some logs," Pinto said, turning toward the woodpile.

"That'd be welcome," she answered.

After Pinto returned with his arms loaded down with oak lengths, he collected his bedding and turned toward the barn.

"Guess you heard that cackle o' gossips, too, eh?" Truett asked, following Pinto onto the porch.

"No, jus' advice off a friend."

"Noticed you kept a distance tonight," Truett continued. "Some friend! Made the both o' you miserable. Ma spent half the evenin' with a batch of old crones. Should've heard 'em. Told Ma to put you off the farm. Ain't proper you bein' unmarried and her a new widow. Shoot, Pa's been buried half a year now. Didn't notice an[illegible] of them comin' by to offer any hands with harvest."

"Can't have yer good name dragged 'round, Tru," Pinto [illegible]tered. "You felt de same 'fore that snow."

"Maybe that's why I know it's wrong. What'll you do, g[illegible] in the barn? Figure that'll stop the talk?"

"It won't," Elsie said, joining them. "People believe [illegible]'ve a mind to. Can you believe it? Ryan, my own cous[illegible]band, asked if you'd taken liberties!"

"Might be bes' if I was to move on."

"Best for whom?" she snapped. "Not for us. Now turn around and get yourself back inside. Christmas mornin' is comin' along, and I won't have discord in my house on a day meant to celebrate peace. Hear?"

"Yes, Ma," Truett said, taking Pinto's bedding and stepping back through the door.

"Pinto?" she asked.

"Got a thing or two in de barn to get," he told her. "I'll do what you think bes', Elsie, but I worry after it."

"Don't. I haven't had so much attention since Tully courted me. I wasn't but fifteen then, you know. Tru'll be fifteen next month. That's half a lifetime."

"Sure, I know," Pinto confessed. More'n half fer some, he thought, remembering Jamie Haskell's pallid face.

* * *

Christmas morning came early. Long before even a crack of dawn appeared on the eastern horizon, Winnie was running around, rousing her brothers.

"Bet there'll be presents," she cried. "Lots of 'em."

"Hush and go back to sleep," Ben grumbled. Brax, on the other hand, threw off his blanket and hurried to get dressed.

"We'll get some breakfast goin'," the younger boy told his sister. "Fryin' bacon'll rouse even Tru!"

So it did, too. Crackling grease might torment the ears, but the wondrous scent of bacon browning on a griddle overpowered even Pinto's resistance. Elsie complained it was too early, but she nevertheless got into some clothes and took over the cooking chores. Pinto scrambled into his trousers and helped Truett roll up the bedding. The two of them near had to roll up Ben along with the blankets.

"I was just havin' myself the best kind o' dream," the twelve-year-old lamented. "Prettiest little gal was . . ."

"Don't get yourself in a lather, little brother," Truett advised. "And don't let Ma hear you havin' impure thoughts on a holy day."

"Yeah, that'd have a sharp edge to it, sure," Ben agreed. By the time Ben had his clothes on and the bedding was stashed away, Elsie called out the food was ready, and the family plus hireling collected themselves for a warming farm breakfast.

The bacon and eggs chased the bite from the frigid air, and the company warmed Pinto's insides. It had been a long time since he'd witnessed the anxious eyes of children eager to see what bounty Christmas morning might shower on them.

First, though, Elsie had the dishes cleared away and scrubbed clean. Then she lit some candles and opened a Bible.

"Ma's never one to miss a chance at seein' verses shared," Ben told Pinto. "But she's not one to stretch it out like some I heard of."

"Not like that preacher fellow last eve," Brax added. "I thought my rump'd fall off if I had to sit on that rail bench another minute."

Pinto couldn't help laughing at Braxton's pained expression. And as it turned out Elsie didn't insist on any elongated reading.

"Only proper to reflect on the meanin' o' this day," she said when she closed the book. "Even if I know you children think it's to round up all the loot north of Mexico."

The little ones laughed heartily, and even Truett cracked a smile. Each person then rushed off to dig gifts out of their secret caches. Then they gathered around the fire and handed out presents.

Elsie had been on the practical side that year, buying cloth and sewing the boys shirts and trousers. Winnie had two new dresses. A new pair of shoes for each was promised on the next journey into Decatur. Truett had used a piece of his trail wages to buy up trinkets in Kansas. Ben and Brax shared a train carved of wooden blocks, and Winnie received a rag doll decked out in a fine blue gingham dress.

For Elsie, Truett had managed a silver heart-shaped locket.

"I never saw anything so lovely unless maybe it was your face the instant you were born, Truett," she said, holding the young man close and hugging him tightly. "I'll treasure it always."

When it was Pinto's turn, he handed out coonskin caps for Ben and Brax, then passed the soft rabbit fur gloves to the womenfolk. He ignored a frowning Truett for a few moments, then could stand it no longer.

"Look here," Pinto said, dragging the saddlebags from beneath the stacked bedding. "Man needs a proper oudfit if he's to take de trail to Kansas."

"Thanks, Pinto," Truett said, examining the carefully tooled leather.

"Never saw anything to top that," Ben observed. "Jared don't even have the like."

"Were a few hours went into it," Elsie said, smiling at Truett's trembling hands. The fourteen-year-old managed a hoarse "thank you," then gripped Pinto's hand firmly.

"Was a pa's chore, dis, and I hope you don't hold it agains' me makin' 'em," Pinto whispered. "Got no boy o' my own, though, you see, and I felt de need."

"Feel it, too," Truett confessed as he leaned against Pinto's solid shoulder. "And I don't judge Pa'd mind."

"No, he'd thank you for it," Elsie added. "Ben, go find Pinto's present now, will you?"

"I'll help," Winnie cried, following Ben into the back room. They emerged with a huge buffalo-hide coat the equal for warmth of anything to be found south of the Dakotas.

"Where . . ." Ben began.

"Ryan brought it out from his last trip out to Fort Griffin," Elsie explained. "You should have bought one yourself instead of picking up that Winchester. It's a coat to last a few winters."

"Bes' I ever owned," Pinto said, putting it on. "Man with a coat like this'd consider himself middlin' well off."

"Only middlin'?" Brax asked.

"'Bout all de Lord'll allow a Texan," Pinto said. "Anything more and he sends down a twisder to take off his roof or a fire to burn his grass."

"Bet you're warm enough now," Winnie said as she wrapped her arms around the waist of the hairy coat.

"Warm as ever I been," Pinto said, resting his hand on her slight shoulder.

Chapter 17

December soon faded into memory. January and February brought more freezing winter mornings and bleak twilights. In spite of the chill air, Pinto insisted on returning to the barn loft. The place was bitter cold and terribly silent, especially when laughter and singing drifted across from the Oakes house. Sometimes, though, Ben would come over and blow up a tune on his mouth organ. The cheering notes always fended off the dreariness, even when the wind took to howling its worst.

Those first months of 1874 saw a rare calm come to the frontier. The cavalry had ridden the Comanches out west for the most part, and the biggest news out of Defiance was that Mary Johnson had run off with a cardsharp out of Waco. Up at the Oakes place, Elsie was kept busy baking birthday cakes. Truett turned fifteen in January, while Ben and Brax each celebrated another year in February. Winifred turned nine March second, Texas Independence Day.

"A birthday's enough cause for celebration," Elsie announced at dinner the day before. "But Texas got itself born March second, too.

I suppose it's fittin' we should have a dance and all to remember that. People've grown tired of Yankee judges and bluecoat cavalry that can't even keep outlaws out of our towns."

"Ain't you heard, Ma?" Truett asked. "Them Hannigans got 'emselves caught up in Kansas. Hung the whole bunch as I heard it."

"Well, there's only fifty others as bad to take their place," Elsie muttered. "Anyhow, Defiance is hostin' a dance, and I think maybe we should go. J. B. Dotham asked if we'd offer 'em a steer, and I agreed."

"Seems they might try some o' the folks can better spare one," Tru grumbled.

"They did," she replied. "But from what I hear they've invited folks in from all over. Plan to feed three, four hundred people. We won't miss one steer much."

"'Sides, we'll eat our share," Ben said, grinning. "How'll that be, Winnie? Instead o' some little birthday cake, you'll have whole tables of pies and cookies. Bet Arabella'll make up a tray of them star tarts. Mmmm. Can taste 'em now."

The youngsters thereupon launched a discussion of which treat made by which neighbor was most favored. Pinto smiled and shook his head. Then Elsie motioned him outside.

"You wouldn't dance last time," she reminded him as they strolled along the porch. "It's closin' in on a year's time you've been with us. Don't you think that entitles me to favors now and then?"

"It's a rocky trail to head down," Pinto warned.

"I've known hardships aplenty, Pinto. And faced 'em head on, every last one."

"You don't half know me."

"Don't I?"

Pinto trembled slightly as she took his hands in her own. A deep longing surfaced in her eyes, and he thought to draw her closer. Something kept him away, though. Words! What had Dotham said at Christmas? So many things.

"You'll at least share the dancin', won't you?" she whispered.

"Figure it to stop there?"

"If it has to," she answered. "You know how fond I've grown of you."

"I know you think you are," he replied. "But there's a hundred things you don't know 'bout."

"I'm listenin'."

"That's jus' it. I can't share it all."

"Then it doesn't merit talkin' about," she argued. "First the dance. There'll be time later for anything else needs attendin'."

"Fair enough," Pinto agreed.

So it was that they prepared for the journey into Defiance. Once again Truett begged the loan of a wagon from the Richardsons for the trip. Pinto took charge of the driving, and little Winnie sandwiched herself between him and her mother. The boys sprawled out in back, together with assorted baked goods Elsie had determined to bring along.

"There's to be an auction this afternoon," she announced en route. "I think it's a fine chance to pick up a team of mules for the plantin'. Think you can find a likely pair, Pinto?"

"Always some poor farmer gone bus'," Pinto answered. "And then de army sells off mules here and there. Won't be so hard."

"Abel Miller's got a wagon he wants shed of, too," Ben announced. "If we bought it, we wouldn't have to borrow one everytime we went anyplace."

"Only wants ten dollars, too," Truett added. "And he'll bring it by for us. All he needs is a word."

Pinto noticed a smile spread across Elsie's face. Clearly there was a conspiracy here.

"I imagine we can spare ten dollars if Pinto can get us the mules at a bargain," Elsie told the youngsters. "Last team Tully bought he paid fifty for."

"I'll save yer ten dollars and maybe a hair more," Pinto promised. "Buy that wagon."

They devoted the remainder of the journey to a discussion of how much acreage to plant that year. Pinto could only shake his head in dismay to hear the boys talk of clearing rocks and trees and adding twenty more acres. It had stretched them to tend the cornfields last year, and Tully had been there to supervise the planting.

"Seems to me time'd be better spent on de cattle," Pinto finally said. "If Tru goes north, you won't have much help with de corn."

"We'd have you," Ben objected.

"Oh, I wouldn't plan so much on that," Pinto told them. "I'll be out chasin' down ponies by April."

He looked back into three faces lined with knowing grins.

"Thought you'd be out doin' that in August," Ben said, laughing. "Ain't left yet."

No, Pinto thought, and it ain't gettin' any easier to go.

The town of Defiance was astir with excitement that second day of March. Banners draped the front of the mercantile and both saloons proclaiming Texas independent. Oldtimers donned the trim blue coats and hats of the Republican Army. A few veterans of that other, later, war appeared in tattered gray as well.

"You should've worn yer old uniform, Pinto," Truett declared.

"Never had much of a uniform," Pinto explained. "Jus' an old coat dyed butternut brown and some wool trousers homespun by some lady down Houston way. Wasn't but rags by firs' winter, and I picked up odds and ends thereafter. Had some pants taken off a Yank toward de end and a shirt passed down from one friend to another and so on till my turn come. No shoes at all!"

"Sounds like us come summer," Brax remarked. "'Course you don't need a lot of clothes in Texas when the sun's blazin' down."

"That heat can be a downright vexation," Pinto observed. "Missed it up Virginia way, though. Colder'n sin up there!"

"That's about enough remembering for now!" Elsie scolded when Pinto drew the wagon to a halt. "Ben, Truett, help me carry these baked goods over to those tables there. Pinto, why don't you take Braxton along to help pick out the mules. Winnie, you come with me, too. I'll bet we can find you something special for your birthday. What say?"

"Yes, Ma," the little girl replied. Tru and Ben tended the goods. Pinto set the wagon brake and led Braxton down the street toward the auction corral. In short order they were inspecting mules and ponies.

As it happened, Pinto found only one team up to the work, and it took nearly two hours of haggling before the owner agreed to part with them for the offered amount. Of course the news that mules were going for twelve dollars at auction made Pinto's offer more palatable.

Ben and Truett, meanwhile, tracked down Abel Miller and purchased the wagon. They also managed to join in a prank or two, for half the children in Wise County had been set loose in Defiance that day.

After tying the mules to the borrowed Richardson wagon, Pinto waved Brax into the crowd of youngsters. He himself was soon dragged over to a large tent by Elsie.

"I'd almost given up on you," she scolded. "Grandpa Jones was beginnin' to feel lucky."

"Jus' finished de hagglin'," Pinto explained. "Now find us a square to join."

As it turned out, a couple out from Weatherford had worn down, and they gladly yielded their spot to Elsie and Pinto. Square dancing wasn't his favorite thing on earth, but Pinto nevertheless held his own, bowing and promenading and swinging. Elsie, on the other hand, was a true wonder. Light on her feet and quick enough to make up for a partner's mistakes, she pranced gracefully at his side as if born there.

"Now I know why you wanted to dance," he told her when they finally left the arena breathless and exhausted. "Got some mean feet, Elsie Oakes."

"Feet hungry for dancin'," she explained. "Tully didn't look it, but he could stomp up a storm. He got heavy those last years, and he didn't find much time for amusement. More's the pity, for he might as well have enjoyed himself some more. Didn't die rich."

"Look there," Pinto said, pointing to a new square forming.

"Guess it's in the blood," Elsie remarked as she spied Truett leading Emily Blasingame. More surprising was the sight of half-pint Ben beside a willowy girl at least a foot taller.

"Now that's a sight," Pinto said, slapping his knee.

"Miranda Phipps," Elsie explained. "She's only four months older, but she got her growin' early. Pa's the blacksmith in Decatur."

"Poor Ben," Pinto said, fighting to hold back the laughter. "Hope she won't swing him too hard. Be a time gettin' him off the handle o' yon Big Dipper."

"Hush," she said.

In truth, Pinto need not add his own jests. Brax and Winnie were doing a fine job of taunting and tormenting their brothers. First Tru and later Ben hollered warnings, but it wasn't until Miranda waved a fist that the younger Oakeses retreated.

"You two seem particular pleased tonight," Ryan Richardson said as he stepped over. "Lowery, do you suppose I might have a word with you alone?"

"Anything I can't hear?" Elsie asked.

"No, I suppose not," Richardson replied. "It's just, well, I don't see how you can get a crop put in out there. Not with Tully gone and all. Be powerful hard on you."

"When's life out here ever been easy?" Elsie asked.

"She's got her heart set on it," Pinto added.

"You know, J. B. and I were talkin' about how short we are of ponies," Richardson told them. "Need twenty before headin' north. Maybe more. I was wonderin' if you might care to supply 'em?"

"Buy for you?" Pinto asked.

"Or run 'em down on the Llano. Either way, we'd be generous employers."

"Why?" Pinto asked. "You know, I counted three, four, good ponies you passed on at de auction. 'Sides, I got a job."

"What is it you want to say, Ryan?" Elsie asked.

"You know people've been talkin'," Richardson confessed. "A lot. Elsie, you're family. I've been doin' a lot of thinkin' on things of late. Arabella's got it in her head she wants to go to finishing school down in Austin. I'd need somebody to run my house. Our boys are near brothers anyhow. Why not sell me your place and move over to the house?"

"As what?" Elsie asked. "Housekeeper? I seem that hard up?"

"Might be more in time," Richardson suggested, gazing nervously at Pinto.

"Ryan, you've been a good friend," Elsie told the rancher, "but I've grown used to bein' independent."

"Then give up the place and set up shop in town. You know the mercantile's up for sale. It's not turned a profit since the Johnson girl ran off. You could move Winnie and the boys to town, give them a chance at a proper education."

"How's that?" she asked. "You see a schoolhouse hereabouts?"

"You know what I mean."

"I'm afraid I don't," Elsie barked. "I'm no town girl, Ryan. I know cornstalks and chickens. I'll stay it out with my boys. They learn what's important as is. In town there'd be temptations I couldn't battle."

"And the plantin'? Tendin' the crop? Who's to do that?" Richardson asked.

"We'll manage," she declared.

"With his help?" Richardson exclaimed. "You know he'll ride off to chase ponies any day. Men like that don't last anywhere."

"I'd judge that'd be my lookout," Pinto growled. "You made yer offer, and I thank you fer what kindness you showed us in de pas'. Maybe you'd bes' leave now 'fore I go to losin' my temper."

"Elsie?" Richardson called.

"You heard Pinto," she answered. "He's better at holding his temper than I am. Go before I let loose a right hand guaranteed to cost you a pair of teeth!"

Richardson started to reply, but the color in Elsie's face had risen, and the rancher threw his arms in the air and stomped away.

She then rested her head on Pinto's shoulder, and he held her a moment. Two women nearby whispered, and one pointed blatantly. Several others quickly collected, and Pinto stepped away.

"It's my doin'," he said, gazing at the ground. "I took too many liberties."

"Nonsense," Elsie argued. "You never did a thing I didn't welcome."

"You don't unnerstand, Elsie. It's not you findin' a man. It's me! If you took to Richardson dere, folks'd be happy fer you. But me? I ain't but a patchwork quilt, a bunch o' cow leavin's somebody's romped on too much. Bes' excuse me now. I done 'nough harm fer one day."

He didn't see Elsie again until it was time to head home. Mostly he'd hung around the wagon, looking after the mules. He hadn't been so far away to miss the gossip mumbled nearby.

"There he is there," a woman might say. "The hired man, Lowery. I heard . . ."

The last part might be about Elsie, or it might be about consorting with Indians. It was startling how many rumors could grow from a simple thing. Each one of them hurt worse than a Comanche lance would have.

Pinto spoke of it neither on the way home nor in the days that followed. He was out in the fields from dawn to dusk, breaking sod or clearing rock. He returned at day's end bent over with weariness. He didn't complain, though. Truett and Ben worked the other mule those same long hours. Brax and Winnie were out with their mother, alternately tossing seed and spreading manure.

The only relief came on those rare occasions when they splashed into the creek and washed away their fatigue in the chill water.

"Never knew I had so many places to get sore," Truett remarked.

"Nor me," Pinto said, collapsing in the shallows. "Give me a range pony to break anytime."

"Might be better if we rode out and roped us some," Truett said, grinning. "Good ponies are fetchin' a high price, what with cattle roundup time nearin'. And who knows what corn'll bring?"

"Better come dear this year," Pinto said, rubbing his shoulders. "Now we got mos' of it in de ground, too late to think o' mustangin'."

"Maybe so," Truett confessed.

"Now lookee there," Pinto said, smiling as he waved Truett closer. "What do you know?"

"Somethin' wrong?" the young man asked anxiously. "Don't got leeches on me, do I?"

"No, somethin' else," Pinto said, touching a finger to the corners of Truett's lip. "Gone and grown a moustache."

"Yeah, been expectin' somebody to notice," Truett said, standing stiff and straight. "Chin hairs, too."

"Oh, that ain't so much," Ben muttered.

"Be shavin' 'fore long," Pinto declared. "Mighty big thing if you ask me."

"I'll be shavin', too," Ben boasted.

"Yeah?" Truett asked. "Shavin' what? The fuzz on your legs?"

"That'll cost you," Ben screamed, charging his brother with fury in his eyes. Truett fended off the raining blows until one finally landed on the whiskered chin. Then the two elder Oakes boys erupted in a short exchange of fists that left Ben's nose and eye puffed up and Truett's chin dented. Meanwhile Brax managed to run off with his battling brothers' clothes.

"Now that's a fool thing to fight over," the eleven-year-old shouted from the cover of a tall willow. "Be a time explainin' to

Ma how you come to bloody each other. Not to mention walkin' all the way to the house bone naked."

It was a mistake. Battered and weary, Brax's taunts ignited fresh fire in his bothers. It was all Pinto could do to keep Truett from skinning Braxton with a knife. And Ben was for hanging the fool.

"You'd figure de work'd leave you three too tired fer such tomfoolery," Pinto scolded them.

"Got to admit one thing, Pinto," Truett said. "Nothin' like a romp or a fight to bring on a laugh."

And it was, Pinto decided, laughter which was the one salve for the worst misery.

Chapter 18

It took most of March, but the plowing finally did get done. Of course, that was but the first step in the long process of bringing corn to harvest. Even so, Pinto felt no small amount of satisfaction when he gazed out on the neat rows of cornfield. Even a mustanger had enough imagination to envision the tall amber stalks that would yield ear after ear come early autumn.

"For a man who says he's no farmer, you did a fair job of it," Elsie told him. "I've been doin' some thinkin'."

"Have you?" Pinto asked.

"Winnie could move in with me permanent. She's hardly been in her little room off the kitchen since Tully passed on. Wouldn't take much to add a few feet to the back of that room. There'd be less room than you've got in the loft, but it'd have you back in the house with us."

"I don't see how that would do, Elsie."

"You could stay there, or else maybe Ben and Brax would take it. You could share the big room with Tru. You two get along fine nowadays. Either way you choose. Or else if you'd like, Winnie and the boys could stay put, and you could—"

"Elsie, bes' hold up right dere," Pinto interrupted. "That'd mean a weddin', you know."

"Find that thought so hard to stomach, do you, Pinto Lowery?"

"Never been much for settlin' in one place too long," he reminded her. "You got boys and little Winnie to grow."

"Takes a steady hand on the reins to get youngsters to the end of the right trail," she told him.

"Yer steady 'nough," he argued. "I jus' been hangin' on here days now, tryin' to figure a way to pull out. Time I was chasin' ponies up de Brazos. Been a while gettin' goin', you know."

"Thought on it hard, have you?" she asked. "Have you considered maybe that's not what you want to do?"

"I'd be lyin' to tell you I ain't found somethin' fine here this winter. Firs' time since I can remember that I knew a place to call home. But I'm nobody to sink roots. And nobody to go countin' on, Elsie. Sooner or later I'll get to feelin' roofed in, and I'll have to ride."

"Seems to me it would have happened already if that was true."

"Wish I could half believe different. Really do. But I know myself better'n you do. It's a better man I'd see you take as a husband dis time 'round. I'd prove a disappointment, jus' like ole Tully. Ain't sure I could abide that."

"You're certain?"

"Ain't nobody ever certain," Pinto said, resting his chin on his chest. "I only know to trus' what's happened before to happen again. Been folks trusted me before. I let 'em down each and every time. No more. It'd mean too much dis time."

She intertwined her fingers with his own, and Pinto's heart skipped a beat. There was a yearning inside him just then, and he only barely fought it off.

"Might be bes' fer me to go tomorrow," he announced. "Give me time to gather my things tonight and say my good-byes come mornin'. Time yet to run in some horses."

He meandered on a quarter hour, but he knew Elsie wasn't listening. She just stood at his side, searching his eyes for a response to her unspoken pleas. He steeled himself against emotion, though, and after a bit she returned to the house. He walked back later, alone with his thoughts.

He announced his leaving to the children after supper that night. Truett nodded sadly. Winnie cried openly, and she wouldn't quiet until Pinto agreed to rock her on his knee.

Later, up in the loft, Ben and Brax appeared.

"You can't go," Ben declared matter-of-factly. "Cousin Ryan's told Tru he can go north again this summer, and we'll need you here."

"Won't even Jared be 'round to keep a watch on us," Brax added. "We done some figurin'. Maybe if Ben and I was to go with you huntin' horses, we'd have it all finished early so you could help tend the cornplants come summer."

"Sure," Ben said, grinning. "We'd make a regular horse-huntin' outfit!"

"And I been practicin' my ropin' real hard, Pinto," Brax said. "I ain't got chin whiskers and such, but I can ride. Your big black even lets me sit atop him."

"I still got my mouth organ," Ben pointed out. As he blew a trail song, Pinto paled. For an instant, there in the dark, it seemed as if Muley Bryant had come back from the dead.

"You all right, Pinto?" Brax asked, touching his hand to Pinto's clammy forehead. "You appear sick."

"Can't go anywhere if you're feverish," Ben said in an almost cheerful voice. "I'll fetch Ma."

"I'm fine," Pinto insisted. "Was only rememberin'. Look, boys, I appreciate yer offer. It's generous to a fault. But where I'll be headin's no place fer boys. Stay here and get some growin' done."

"You'll come back when you get the horses caught?" Ben asked.

"Got to sell 'em, don't I?" Pinto asked. "Anyhow, I wouldn't jus' ride off and never see friends again. Not 'less somethin' come along and blew me off to Kansas or Wes' Texas, or maybe Colorado Terridory."

"Ma'll miss you bad," Ben declared. "Winnie, too."

"And you?" Pinto asked.

"I won't have no big black horse to feed," Brax mumbled. "Nor anybody to spin stories in the loft."

The eleven-year-old collapsed against Pinto's side. A tear cascaded down the boy's cheek and fell on Pinto's wrist.

"Be missin' you boys, too," Pinto confessed as Ben edged closer. "But you'll do fine. Got de makin's o' good men in you."

Ben held his mouth organ to his lips and tried to manage a melody. The lips quivered, and a sort of unharmonic sob came out.

"Can't take me to heart, you know," Pinto whispered. "All I ever was's a bit o' wind blew through off de Llano. Be forgot in a year."

"You're wrong, Pinto," Ben said, rubbing his eyes dry. "Not ever forgot."

"Not ever," Brax echoed.

"Nor you, boys," Pinto said, pulling them close for a moment. And knowing it would be better for all of them if it wasn't so.

He thought to leave before breakfast that next morning, but Elsie was up earlier than usual, and Ben appeared with the Winchester to insure Pinto didn't escape.

"Plan to shoot me, Ben?" Pinto cried in surprise.

"Brax asked Ma if maybe we could hole you in the foot. Not enough to cripple or anything. Just enough to keep you here. She said you were old enough to make up your own mind."

"What do you figure?" Pinto asked as Ben relaxed his grip and let the rifle's barrel drop toward the ground.

"Don't mean you come to the right choice, just cause you're grown. Better for everybody if you was to stay."

"Can't," Pinto declared.

"Then I don't suppose a rifle'd hold you. 'Specially not one without any bullets in it. But you can come eat some breakfast. Fresh sausage and blueberry muffins. Mexican omelet."

"Hurryin' me on my way, eh?"

"Stuffin' you so you won't starve 'fore May's out."

Pinto followed Ben to the house and washed his face and hands as he'd done a hundred times before. The breakfast was as tasty as any he'd ever eaten, and he lauded Elsie's efforts.

"She had a lot o' time to work on it," Winnie explained. "We didn't sleep much last night."

The six of them sat silently around the table then for close to a quarter hour. Finally Pinto rose and started for the door.

"Here," Elsie called, offering a flour sack of food.

"Don't go," Winnie cried, clamping hold of one leg.

"We all of us want you to stay," Truett announced. "But only if you want. Ain't any obligation owed us. And we thank you for what you done already."

"Yeah," Ben agreed.

It was likely rehearsed, and Pinto nodded his own thanks to Elsie for easing his escape. Nevertheless, after prying Winnie's fingers loose, he felt ten eyes on his back all the way to the corral. The big black was already saddled, and all Pinto had to do was tie his belongings atop the pack horse.

"You'll visit when you pass nearby, won't you?" Elsie called.

"Lightnin' strike me dead if I don't," Pinto answered. Then he pulled the gate open and led out the horses. In another instant he was mounted and riding west.

Pinto Lowery was three days reaching open country. Passing through the scattered towns and ranches north of the Brazos, listening to the shouts of children swimming the river or mothers announcing supper ready, he was constantly reminded of the life he had just put behind him.

"Can't run forever, boys," Captain Maven had said the morning they'd laid down their arms at Appomattox. "Sooner or later a man's got to make his stand, fight it out, and go home again."

The words had rung hollow for what was left of the Marshall Guards. Home was a place left a thousand and a half miles behind. Who knew if the town still stood? And if it did, what man among them who'd left as a fuzz-cheeked child could return, scarred and bitter, to what he'd known before?

Once Pinto had delighted in the windswept plain and rock-studded hills of western Texas. Now the country was filling up with people, cows, and towns. He found few signs of mustangs, and when he did run down a pair of horses, they proved to be wearing Hood County brands.

"Comanche-stolen mos' likely," Pinto grumbled. He left the animals in Palo Pinto in hopes their owner might fetch them.

"Might be they'd pay a reward," Krug Mannion, the liveryman, explained.

"If they offer one, get 'em do send it to Elsie Oakes out in Defiance."

"Family?" Mannion asked. "Didn't know you to have none."

"Jus' tell 'em, won't you?" Pinto replied sharply.

"No skin off my chin either way, Lowery. Man comes to need family now and again, though," Mannion added. Reading Pinto's frown, the liveryman added, "Only makin' conversation."

"Didn't come lookin' fer any o' that," Pinto barked. "Be on my way now."

He rode off slowly, knowing Mannion was sure to laugh at the notion that a vagabond mustanger like Pinto Lowery should ever find a home. Yes, it was crazed idea. And yet Pinto saw Elsie and the children in every shadow, every dream. No matter how far he rode, he couldn't manage to shake the memory of that final farewell.

It was near the middle of April when Pinto finally came across mustangs. By then he was way up north of Buffalo Springs, near where the Little Wichita emptied into the Red River. Across to the north the Chickasaw traders always had horses to swap, and if worst came to worst, Pinto supposed he might pick up a few raw ponies and break them into proper trail mounts before turning south to Wise County.

"Maybe little ole Brax can even take a crack at one," Pinto said, laughing as he envisioned the boy, yellow hair flying in all directions, battling to stay atop of a Chickasaw pony.

The white-faced stallion snorted and stomped as its rider lost his sense of direction.

"Can't help it, boy," Pinto told the horse. "Ain't no escapin' their faces, it seems."

Of course, the stallion wasn't the least interested in Pinto's daydreams. The big horse had sniffed out its fellow creatures, and it now bolted across the low hills with rare abandon. Pinto gave a backward glance at his packhorse and held on tightly as he was jolted and jarred. He knew it was best to give the horse its head. After all, if there were mustangs close by, the black would run them down.

As it happened, the stallion raced into the midst of a small herd. Pinto counted twenty or thirty, and there were more besides. At first the animals shied away, but weeks in the open had wrung most of the human scent out of Pinto, and the lathered black was fast at work befriending mares.

"Don't know whether you'll bring 'em along or dey'll have you ridin' off," Pinto declared as he pulled the stallion away. "Time we made some plans."

Pinto's withdrawal was timely, for a buckskin stallion came running over moments later, snorting at the intruder that dared approach his harem.

"Not now, boy," Pinto said as he fought to hold the big black in check. "I'll be wantin' more'n a bloody horse fer my trouble."

And so, after retrieving the wandering packhorse from the grassland to the south, Pinto set about making plans. For the first time in days he was his old self, jabbering away about mustangs and searching out a hollow to serve as the jaws of a horse trap. He wasn't lucky enough to find the sort of box canyon that had served so well on the Brazos, but he did locate a steep ravine. In three days of sweat and agony Pinto erected fences walling off a thirty foot stretch on both ends. He slid the rails aside on the west end and double-lashed the ones on the east side. Finally he climbed atop the black stallion and set out to capture the buckskin's harem.

Pinto knew from the first he would never capture the whole batch. For one thing, the buckskin wasn't half as dominant as the black had been. A dozen other stallions ran with the herd, and many of them clearly had a mare or two to themselves.

"Be lucky to come up with three dozen," Pinto told himself. Or two. But even ten good saddle horses would turn a handsome profit. And in the back of his mind crept the notion to save the best three mares and do a bit of breeding.

"You'd cooperate, wouldn't you, boy?" Pinto asked the stallion. The big horse snorted its response, and Pinto urged the animal into a gallop. In less than an hour's riding, horse and rider were closing in on the mustangs from the northwest.

"Yah!" Pinto hollered as he waved a blanket and set the horses running. "Yah!"

Instantly the mustangs took flight. As feared, a stallion here and there broke away with a mare or two. But many of the mares nursed colts or fillies, and they wouldn't abandon a young one, not even for the lure of freedom.

Pinto concentrated on the buckskin. The black closed on its rival with rare fury, and Pinto threw a rope over the tan horse and led it along. That buckskin, lathered and fiery-eyed, chortled and fumed as it ran along, held captive by Pinto's braided lariat.

Running at full gallop, the stampeding horses covered the distance to the ravine in a third of the time it had taken Pinto to ride north earlier that morning. As the bare fenceposts loomed close, Pinto released his grip on the lariat and left the buckskin to shoot ahead. Now trapped by the press of other horses, the stallion was forced past the makeshift corral along with those that hadn't split off from the harem. When the last colt galloped past, Pinto leaped to the ground and hurried to slide the rails into place. He was securing the final two when the buckskin, seeing the eastern edge of the ravine barred, turned to challenge the west end.

"No, yer a hair too late," Pinto called to the frustrated horse. "Jus' as well. Bet you'd ended up Chickasaw trade goods or else table meat come winter. I won't work de spirit out o' you, nor use a geldin' knife."

Pinto sat atop the rail fence the rest of that morning, mentally noting each horse in turn. He counted five stallions besides the buckskin. Three of them were full grown and sure to make good cow ponies. Two were barely more than yearlings and would want some growing. Of the sixteen mares, four were smart-looking and sure to breed fine ponies. Three of the others were branded, and Pinto cursed that for bad luck. He'd have a time managing more than ten mounts for Ryan Richardson and J. B. Dotham. Of the remainder, eight were colts and six were fillies. Near half the animals, in other words, would want rearing.

"Fine beginnin' fer a breeder," Pinto noted, "but not any too promisin' for a trader."

Maybe it was fate's way of edging Pinto Lowery toward a settled life. Or the big black's revenge for breaking him to saddle. Whatever, Pinto set to work gentling the stallions and working the edge off the mares. He didn't bother with the younger horses. Once their mamas were pliable, they wouldn't run, and the littler mustangs would make no break on their own.

The same day Pinto managed to stay atop the buckskin and race the animal three times around the corral, he shot a goose and turned the big bird on a spit. He was in rare good humor, and he passed the cooking time whistling old camp tunes and watching the big black frolic with the mares.

Suddenly the wind died away, leaving an unearthly quiet to haunt the hillside.

"Never knew silence to have an echo," he said, feeling cold in spite of a blistering afternoon sun.

Gazing at the mares nuzzling their young or at the white-faced stallion cavorting, he felt terribly empty and more alone than since that first night a lifetime before when he'd marched off to Confederate service and left his ash-faced mother behind.

"A man wants company," Jamie had declared as he rolled his blankets out alongside George Lowery. "Else the loneliness plum swallows him whole."

"Ain't it de way!" Pinto called to the horses. And he determined to lead out his small herd next morning, ready or not.

Chapter 19

The move south and east to Wise County covered some forty miles. Along the way one of the stallions and two mares ran off, but all in all Pinto deemed his journey a success. The buckskin was proving as lively, if a bit less durable, than Pinto's big black, and the other horses seemed to have lost most of their wildness.

Once across the Trinity, Pinto began searching out a likely horse camp. West of Decatur and north of Defiance he located a broad grassland abandoned to the wind, save for a few maverick longhorns.

"Guess you've gone and become a rancher, too, Pinto," he told himself once he was satisfied the animals bore no brand. After locating the horses along a well-watered stretch, Pinto led the three branded mares into Decatur. He left them for their owners and bought needed supplies, then inquired after the Oakeses.

"Them corn farmers down south?" the store clerk asked. "Comely sort o' woman with a passel o' kids. Yeah, come through here buyin' some piece goods a few weeks back. Lost her man, I hear. Shows. She was weathered down considerable."

It wasn't what Pinto wanted to hear. Next day he collected two stallions and the six mares that had weaned their young to take to the Double R. He'd long since decided to offer Ben Oakes the buckskin for a saddle horse, and the brood mares would remain as well, together with the herd of spindle-legged youngsters. One of the yearling stallions had promise, and the other was enough horse to carry little Brax or Winnie about.

Pinto's arrival at the Double R brought a buzz of excitement.

"Thought you were halfway to Colorado sure," Richardson said as he eyed Pinto's string. "And here you were off working up cow ponies the whole time."

"Got some good 'uns, too," Pinto replied. "Dey'll carry a man to Kansas and back again, each and every one of 'em."

"I believe they just might," the rancher agreed. He then inspected the animals personally before locating Jared and a pair of cowboys. "Give 'em a ride, boys," Richardson ordered. "See what you think."

Pinto wandered over to a live oak and dismounted. There was a watering trough nearby, and the big black drank thirstily from it.

"Was wonderin' when you'd come back," a familiar voice spoke from the opposite side of the thick-trunked tree.

"That can't be Tru Oakes makin' them man sounds," Pinto said, stepping over and greeting the young man warmly. "Readyin' yerself fer Kansas, I guess."

"Just visitin' Jared," Truett explained. "You got your horses, I see."

"Some," Pinto said. "Mos'ly I got a lot o' stumblefooted colts and fresh-weaned fillies."

"Where?"

"North a ways. Maybe you'll pay a call later on."

"Maybe you'll pay us one."

"Oh, I'll come by when I can," Pinto said, avoiding Tru's probing eyes. "Always meant to keep an eye yer way."

"Ma'd welcome you to supper."

"Thank her, but I got work waitin'."

"I don't see why you don't bring your horses and come along

home," Truett said, stepping closer and looking Pinto squarely in the eye. "You wouldn't have come back if it wasn't in your mind."

"Brought horses to sell," Pinto lied.

"Well, the invite's there for you when you want it," Truett concluded. "Looks like Jared's happy with the horses. Cousin Ryan's sure to offer you top price. Jared's particular."

"Well, dere's that ches'nut mare I sold him to figure in."

"Yeah, he's partial fond of that horse."

Jared met a moment with his father, and the Richardsons, father and son, stepped over to conclude business. Pinto met them, came to terms, and then glanced back to where Truett had waited. The boy was stroking the black stallion, but when Pinto called to him, Truett turned and hurried along toward where Arabella stood on the porch.

"Guess he spoke his piece," Pinto told the stallion as he climbed atop its back.

Pinto Lowery was no stranger to the Oakes farm those next few days. Once each morning and again toward dusk he put the buckskin or one of the mares through its paces. Each time he rode along the rim of the cornfields or up past the house. He watched Elsie hang up laundry or spied on the boys swimming in the river after working the rows of fledgling cornplants. Once or twice Ben or Brax would notice and wave. Pinto always nodded, but he never rode down to visit.

"You'd only go down there once," he told himself. "Wouldn't be able to leave a second time."

It was the last day of May when Truett appeared. The midday sun was hanging high overhead, and Pinto was only just finishing his work with one of the yearlings.

"Howdy!" Truett called.

"Howdy!" Pinto responded. "Seems you took a wrong turn. Double R's south."

"Know it is," Tru answered as he pulled his horse up and

climbed down. "Thought maybe you might not have gotten around to eatin'. Ma packed some ham and biscuits. Part of a peach cobbler, too."

"It'd be a welcome change from jerked beef and prairie hen," Pinto confessed. "Come along and sit yerself at my table here. Pull up a chair."

Truett stared at the barren ground and laughed. He then drew a provision bag from his saddlebags and walked over and joined Pinto beneath a pair of live oaks.

"You know Ben'll take after me with a scalpin' knife when he finds out about this," Truett said, opening up the bag and doling out the food. "He's been after me better'n a week to take him up here. I figure he's eager to ask the loan of a horse."

"See that buckskin?" Pinto asked as he stuffed slices of ham between two biscuits. "Been gettin' him ready fer Ben."

"Lot of horse for a boy, don't you think?" Truett asked.

"You felt like a boy much lately, Tru? Hard to see a little brother gettin' bigger, but Ben's thirteen now. I considered givin' over de buckskin to you and passin' yer horse along, but den . . ."

"Ben's been his whole life gettin' hand-me-downs," Truett said, nodding. "Been ridin' ole Sugarcane. Better this way. And 'sides, I'm fond of my fool pony, even if it don't seem like much to most folks."

"Well, you get too good-lookin' a horse, somebody jus' comes along and swaps you out o' him. Or takes him when you're not watchin'."

"Nobody's stolen that big black of yours."

"Ain't half a dozen folk even in Texas he won't throw off," Pinto explained.

"Jared told me you did real well sellin' off your horses the other day. Didn't buy this land, did you?"

"No, I'm jus' borrowin' it fer a time. Till dem little 'uns get to be of a size."

"I'd guess that'll take a while."

"Likely will."

"If you was to come back to our place, I'll bet Ben, Brax, and me could help you build a proper work corral."

"You'd be bound fer Kansas soon."

"Maybe," Truett said, frowning. "Maybe not."

"Trouble?"

"Piles of it," Truett explained. "I thought I could take care of things. To think I tried to run you off last fall! Must've been sincerely addled."

"How so?" Pinto asked, resting a hand on the boy's shoulder to calm him.

"First off, I don't do anything right. I tried to add the room out back Ma wants, but I made a mess of it. Planks don't meet where they ought to, and I used twice the nails a fellow who knew what he was doing would've. Nails ain't cheap, you know. They come dear in Defiance and near that bad even in Fort Worth. Not much chance of gettin' there, I can tell you."

"Maybe I'll drop down that way."

"Wouldn't matter now," Truett grumbled. "Jared and his pa came over and tore down the whole thing. Then they started over, and it went up just perfect. See? I can't do anything right!"

"All you did was try. Can't anybody fault that."

"There's the cornfields, too. I can't seem to keep Ben and Brax at the hoein' nor do it myself, either. It's hot, and some of the plants are near scorched. At dinner Ben goes to talkin' how you kept 'em green last summer, and you wasn't even farmbred. Well, I suppose you know what that makes me."

"I don't figure yer ma took it much to heart, Tru."

"No, she never does. But it ain't lost on her, neither. Cousin Ryan come by to talk over the cattle drive. Shoot, how was I to know we're supposed to round up our own stock, brand the yearlings, cut the bull calves. Pinto, I never done that. Don't know as I can. Jared says it's not so much, but I never even cut an ear notch, much less . . ."

"Sure," Pinto said, laughing. "Wasn't a cowboy born didn't feel it. Maybe I'll happen along and show you how it's done."

"Never branded anything either."

"Got a job o' that to do my own self. Could be we could mark these ponies and yer calves at de same time."

"There's so much more, too. We need your help all the time, not such with a bit of brandin' and geldin'."

"You'll manage," Pinto assured the young man.

"I'm not a man yet, Pinto. I got a lot of growin' yet to get done. Ben, too, and Brax. Winnie misses you, and Ma . . ."

"Give me a lissen here," Pinto said, steadying Truett a second time. "Not a man you say? Shoot, you look one to me. Soon 'nough you'll be taller, too. But manliness ain't comin' with de size. It's inside, here," Pinto said, jabbing a finger into his own chest. "Hard times'll grow you up faster'n anybody'd wish. Guess it's nature's way o' seein' to things. Don't sell yerself short jus' yet. Ole Richardson's not settin' out north fer a week or so, and we'll figure out a way to get yer cows ready by then."

"You mean to stay out here all alone?"

"Alone?" Pinto asked. "Got all these ponies 'round. Ain't much alone."

But Truett stared hard. There was no fooling that boy. Even as young Oakes handed over a square of cobbler wrapped in a napkin, he remained unconvinced.

"There's different kinds of bein' alone," Truett declared. "I've known every one of 'em since Pa died. Don't tell me different, Pinto. I know."

After Truett's visit, Pinto received company regularly. The first week of June he presented the buckskin to Ben, and a day later brought a spotted stallion by for Brax and two gentle mares bought off a Decatur farmer.

"Now you'll be all o' you mounted," he told Winnie as the girl climbed atop hers. "Other's fer yer ma. Figure Sugarcane to need a res'."

"Oh?" Elsie asked. "And just how will we pay for all this good fortune?"

"Figure you to keep me stocked up on cobbler and cornmeal," Pinto replied. "You boys try yer hands at throwin' ropes, hear? We got some roundin' up to tend by and by."

"We will," Truett promised. "And the other, too."

"Sure," Pinto said, laughing at the dread looks crossing the littler boys' faces. "By and by."

"You could stay . . . to supper," Elsie suggested as she stepped closer. "We've been a time missin' your company."

"I won't be far," Pinto said, avoiding her eyes. "But I got work to tend jus' now."

In truth they both knew that he'd done about all there was to do with the remaining horses out on the range, and he now devoted most of his time prowling Wise County in search of the odd range pony. He'd roped three, but they weren't much of a challenge and would soon be ready for delivery to J. B. Dotham.

"You know that boy Truett's right," Pinto muttered as he rode back to his camp. "Ain't nothin' holdin' you here."

Truett had been right about the loneliness, too. It plagued Pinto Lowery almost every waking moment.

Chapter 20

Pinto was up early the morning the riders came. He'd been expecting a call from J. B. Dotham, and thus he paid little attention to the half-dozen cowboys who appeared out of the morning mists. Dotham and Richardson rode in the lead, together with a familiar-looking fellow Pinto couldn't quite place. He soon introduced himself.

"Potter Diggs's the name," the man said. "Wise County Sheriff. You're Lowery, I take it."

"I am," Pinto said, anxiously eyeing the lawman's companions. There was an ill-concealed anger on each face. Even Dotham and Richardson, who were usually peaceful types, had their dander up.

"Heard you might be out this way," the sheriff added.

"Well, Mr. Dotham here knows it pretty well. Was supposed do pick up some horses here. Mr. Richardson's done some buyin' off me, too. Ain't done a thing wrong as I know. What's on yer mind?"

"Not you, and that's for sure," one of the cowboys muttered.

"Come to see if maybe you seen some men ride by," Diggs said, searching the horizon. "Have you?"

"Nobody this mornin'," Pinto answered. "Trouble?"

"Robbed the Pratt farm," Dotham explained. "Between here and Decatur."

"Kilt ole Lloyd," a cowboy said, grinding his teeth. "Shot him clean through the head."

"Did in Mary Agnes, too," Richardson said, paling. "Shot two of the kids, then set the house on fire, figurin' the others'd burn inside."

"Ain't seen a soul," Pinto said, swallowing hard. "'Course, I got all these horses here, and they raise a fair cloud o' dus'. Noise, too. Could've a dozen men rode a mile away and come right pas' me."

"Wasn't a dozen," Diggs said, "but might as well be. Got a fair description from Jimmy Pratt. Big man with a busted up face. Joe Hannigan's back."

"Can't be," Pinto said, growing cold inside. "I heard dey hung him up in Kansas."

"Tried," Richardson said as he swung his horse around. "They killed two deputies and made their escape. Got no more time for swappin' tales now. If they rode past you, they just might be headed for my place. Arabella and the boys are there alone!"

"You keep an eye open, Lowery," the sheriff suggested. "Spot 'em, duck for cover and get us word. Never could stomach no one makes a habit o' shootin' females and little kids."

"I'll be lookin'," Pinto told them.

"Could be needin' horses, too," Dotham warned. "Guard your stock."

"Trus' me to do what's needed," Pinto replied.

The posse then turned south and rode off as agitated as before. Pinto poured the remnants of a coffee pot onto the fire and kicked dirt over the coals.

Won't get to Richardson's place firs', Pinto mused. No, they'd come across the Oakes farm. Weren't there good saddle horses in the corral now and nobody but a widow and her kids in the way?

Pinto wasted no time in saddling the black and in loading the Henry's magazine. He filled both pockets with extra cartridges, then climbed atop the stallion and turned south. He didn't bother about the horses. He'd hand Joe Hannigan every blessed one of them if the outlaw would busy himself there and spare Elsie.

When did fate ever deal you a good hand when a poor one was to be had? Pinto wondered. He slapped the black's rump and galloped off toward the little farmhouse that had suddenly become his heart. He recalled Big Nose Joe and grinning Pat, recalled the still, solemn eyes of little Muley Bryant. And in his nightmare imagination, those still eyes belonged to Ben and Brax, to Winifred and Truett. Pat was blowing up a tune on Ben's mouth organ, and Joe was closing in on Elsie.

"No!" Pinto shouted as he raced on. "Not this time!"

A clear-headed man would have ridden with caution. Pinto Lowery had seen enough of war to know how it was best gone about. But just then he was past thinking. A world of fear gripped him, and he was determined not to be too late, not to ride upon Elsie and the children as Richardson, Dotham, and Diggs had found those other poor unfortunates.

He was racing toward the cornfield when a glint of metal caught his eye. He instinctively turned the black away, and it saved his life. Two rifle shots punctuated the summer morning, and a third followed on the heels of the others.

Pinto heard one whine past, and another nicked his right boot. It was the third shot that brought results, though. It exploded in the big black's side and spattered Pinto's leg with blood.

"Lord, I've led you right into 'em, boy," Pinto cried as he felt the stallion stumble onward. He managed to coax the screaming creature into a stand of willows before the animal collapsed in a dying shudder.

"He went into them trees!" someone hollered. "I saw him. You hit him, I think, Pete."

A gangly redhead emerged from the cornfield and dashed toward the trees. Pinto tore the Henry from its scabbard and drew down on the foolhardy outlaw.

"Done with bein' de fool this day," Pinto said, watching the charging figure fill the rifle's sights. It took but a twitch of the finger to send a lead pellet exploding out the barrel of the rifle. The red-head's chin flew back, and he spun crazily. For a second the outlaw teetered on one leg as he tried to hold what was left of his jaw onto his face.

"Pete?" the voice from the cornfield called. Pinto swung his rifle to bear on the second gunman even as the first plunged facedown into the grass, dead. The Henry steadied on a hint of red flannel crawling between the green rows of young cornplants. Pinto worked the rifle's lever, aimed, and fired. The flannel jumped into the air and fell downward, silent.

Pinto didn't know how many there had been, but he was determined to offer them no second easy chance. He paused a moment, drinking in the scene before him. Finally he detected a movement to his right. Horses! Three animals crept slowly toward the wood. Behind them two pairs of human legs kept pace.

"You up there, mister?" a youngish voice called. "Not dead yet, eh? You the papa maybe? Want to bargain some? Here, see what I got to trade."

A ragged man in his mid-twenties stepped out, holding a pistol against the forehead of Ben Oakes.

"That your papa, boy?" the raider asked. "Talk at him?"

"My pa's dead," Ben explained. "For all I know you shot up one of your own men!"

"Ain't no chance o' that, boy. There's the three o' us out here, Joe and Pat at the house, and the cousins watchin' the road. Now, mister, if you give value to this here child, step out so I can see you. Hear?"

Pinto heard just fine. What's more, he read the terror in Ben's eyes. The outlaw was green, though. He held his double-action Colt uncocked. Pinto worked the Henry's lever and readied another shot.

"You ain't killed many men, have you?" Pinto shouted as he stepped from the willows. "Ben, you trus' me?" The boy nodded, and Pinto took aim with the Henry. "Run, Ben!" Pinto shouted.

Ben managed two steps before the outlaw thought to draw the

hammer back with his thumb. Before the Colt drew level with Ben's flying shoulders, Pinto had killed his third man that morning.

"Pinto, he was lyin'!" Ben shouted as he threw himself flat onto the ground. "Behind you!"

Pinto made a quick half turn, working the Henry's lever as he dove for cover. A grim, dark-eyed forty-year-old rested a Winchester on one knee and opened fire, spraying the ground with bullets. Pinto cried in pain as one sliced through his left forearm. Ben screamed. Then a pistol shot ended the madness.

"Pinto?" Ben called as he tore the Colt from his would-be killer's hand and rushed to Pinto's side. "You're hit!"

"Alive, though," Pinto said, not understanding quite how. Then Jared Richardson stepped into view.

"Come lookin' for Pa," the young man explained as he replaced a pistol in its holster. "Heard the shootin'."

"Ben?" Pinto asked, gazing at the pale-faced boy huddling beside him.

"Come an hour ago," Ben explained as he tore off his shirt and began wrapping it around Pinto's bloody arm. "I was off feedin' the hogs. Ma yelled for me to scat, and I lit out o' there pronto. Then these men ride down, shootin' guns, blastin' the house, shatterin' all the windows. These fellows run me down here. That one there," Ben said, pointing to the older outlaw, "was takin' out a knife when you come up. I figure they were goin' to cut my throat."

"And de others?" Pinto asked, wincing as Ben pulled the binding tight and tied it off.

"Ain't any gunfire come from the house in a while now," Jared said, frowning. "Best we get up there and have a look."

"We?" Pinto asked as he stepped over and picked up the Winchester lying beside the nearby corpse. "Ain't a thing fer you to try."

"Figure I'm too young?" Jared said, planting a hand on each hip. "I was old enough to save your hide, Pinto Lowery. Now, how do we go about it."

"Ben," Pinto said, turning to the younger boy.

"I'm comin', too," Ben declared. "It's my family after all."

"Then stay behind me de both o' you," Pinto barked. "And be ready."

Pinto led the way into the willows and out onto the far hillside. As they passed the lifeless stallion, Pinto heard both youngsters groan. Pinto himself dared not look at the poor animal. He'd seen a thousand dead men on the battlefields in Virginia, killed every way a man could be killed, but it was always seeing the cavalry horses lying dead that tore at him.

"Ain't their war," Jamie had remarked once.

"Nor mine, neither," Pinto had answered. "Here we're all o' us fightin' it."

That was how he felt now. Here was a nightmare brought down upon him. He'd killed three outlaws. Outlaws? Not a one had practiced the trade long. Like as not they were out-of-work cowboys.

The ones at the house were different. Pinto knew that instinctively, even if only one was in clear view. A young man wearing baggy overalls over his bare shoulders and bony chest tended three horses. The boy's face was half hidden by a gaudy hat whose huge plume exploded off one side and flowed down the young outlaw's neck.

Pinto glanced around, but he saw no one else. Loud voices inside the house shouted threats, and glass shattered amid a child's scream.

"Pinto?" Ben whimpered.

"Watch that 'un," Pinto said, pointing toward the horse-tender. "Jared, if he goes to movin', you shoot him dead."

"There's more of 'em," Ben warned.

"Some inside," Pinto said, nodding. "More watchin' de road. Stay here with Jared."

"I'm comin'," Ben insisted.

Pinto shook his head and inched his way along the wall of the barn. It was a good thirty feet to the house, though, and all of it was in plain sight of the lookout. Once the boy got the horses tied, he danced over to the privy.

"Now?" Ben asked, snickering.

"Come on," Pinto said grimly. They dashed to the house. Then

Pinto rested the rifles beside the window of the back bedroom. He took his own pistol and the Colt Ben had brought along, then stepped through the open window frame, taking care to avoid the razor-sharp shards of splintered glass.

Ben followed with the rifles. The two of them crawled to the door, then cracked it open. Just ahead Winnie lay on the floor, sobbing. Braxton did what he could to soothe her. Truett lay sprawled on the floor, his face battered and bruised. Big Joe Hannigan towered over Elsie.

"Now any fool can see we mean business, ma'am," Joe yelled. "Want I should have my little brother here open up that little gal there for you? He does it with style, you know. Comanche style. Bit at a time so the screamin' lasts a good while."

"I told you that's all!" Elsie cried. "Take it and go!"

"Oh, we'll do that sure enough," Pat Hannigan added. "Soon's we're sure you ain't held nothin' back."

Pat stepped toward the children. As he drew a knife with one hand, he held Muley Bryant's mouth organ to his lips with the other.

"Pat's right fond o' music," Joe said, laughing. "Does drown out the hollerin' some, though."

"Pinto?" Ben pleaded.

Lord, you lef' me with de short stick again, Pinto thought as he took a deep breath. There was nothing to think over now. Long odds and no time. Pinto sprang forward like a coiled snake, knocking Pat Hannigan back into his brother and opening up with both pistols until all twelve shots had torn the room apart. Yellow tongues of fire leaped from the far side of the powder-choked room, and Pinto's left leg buckled as a bullet shattered the bone.

"Get down!" Pinto shouted as Elsie made a dash for the children. By then Ben had them flattened against the floorboards and shielded with his own bare back.

Elsie crawled over and drew the little ones to her as the smoke began to clear. Pinto hurried to reload his pistols, and Truett dragged himself, moaning, behind the cover of the kitchen stove. Across the room Joe Hannigan slumped in a chair, the top half of his ugly face blown away. A bloody smear marked the doorway where Pat had escaped.

"Elsie, you all right?" Pinto called.

"Better'n you are," Ben answered, frowning at Pinto's bent leg.

"Best let me put a splint on it," Elsie suggested.

"Later," Pinto replied. "There's accounts lef' to clear,"

"Let him go," Elsie urged. "There's been enough death."

"No, I owe that 'un," Pinto said, spitting the bitterness from his mouth as he hopped to the door. Fer Muley, he told himself. And de others who'd cross his path.

Pat was just reaching the woodpile when Pinto spotted him. The younger Hannigan's right hip was a world of blood, and there were two swelling circles of red below the right knee as well.

"Jared?" Pinto shouted.

"I missed," young Richardson answered. Seconds later the third outlaw splintered the doorframe with two well-placed shots from the privy.

"Ben, toss me that rifle," Pinto said, holstering his pistol and setting the second one aside. "Tru, you alive?"

"Dizzy's all," Truett replied. "Pa gave me worse lickin's plenty o' times."

"Take that shotgun off de floor and load her up," Pinto advised. "Then watch de back o' de house. I aim to work de front."

"You're bleedin'!" Elsie complained.

"Don't suppose it'll make de floor much difference. Keep down. Got to settle accounts."

Pinto accepted the Henry from Ben's trembling hands, then inhaled deeply. For several moments there wasn't a hint of Pat Hannigan. Then the arrogant outlaw struck up a tune on the mouth organ.

"I remember you now!" Hannigan bellowed. "That livery a year or so back. I cut down your boy out in the barn, remember?"

"Bad mistake comin' back here," Pinto answered.

"Back?" Pat called.

"Was me found yer camp down at de creek, dropped dem cousins. Was easy, you know. Close to's easy as shootin' Joe's big nose off dis mornin'."

"Joe!" Pat screamed.

"He's gettin' you a place ready in hell," Pinto hollered. "Now come on!"

Pat was angry, but not stupid enough to rush the house with a busted hip. He did, however, lift his head just enough for Pinto to aim a bullet a hair back of the right ear. Pinto squeezed off his shot, but the bullet missed its mark an inch and carried away only half of Pat Hannigan's earlobe.

Pain and fury merged in an instant, and Pat leaped over the woodpile, firing wildly. Bullets shattered plates in a cupboard and pinged off the cast-iron stove. Pinto returned the fire with cool murder in his heart. Two bullets opened up Pat's chest, and a third broke three teeth before driving splinters of bone into the young outlaw's brain. Pat Hannigan screamed in agony and tore at his clothes. Then his eyes rolled back into his head, and he collapsed in the woodpile.

Pinto almost immediately shifted his fire toward the privy, but the slight-shouldered boy had vanished. Pinto half hoped the young outlaw had escaped. He hadn't.

"Best you hold real still, mister," the surviving raider advised as he stepped out of the back room waving his rifle toward Elsie and the children. "Stop!" he ordered as Pinto tried to slide past the door. "Show yourself or I'll kill 'em all, one by one."

"No!" Truett screamed, fumbling with the shotgun. The young bandit fired a round at the stove, and Truett discarded the scattergun.

"Pinto, he'll only kill us anyway," Elsie said, staring at the wild eyes of the gunman.

"All I want's the money," the raider argued. "Give it to me, and I go."

"Sure," Pinto said, hobbling over and prying the banknotes from Joe Hannigan's clenched fist. "Here."

"Drop that rifle first."

"Not likely," Pinto replied, steadying himself as his left leg went numb.

"You got five seconds," the outlaw announced as he grabbed Braxton by the shoulder and slung him to the floor.

Pinto studied his adversary's cold eyes and dropped the Henry. The outlaw then accepted the bills with a laugh of disdain.

"You ain't so much, Joe Hannigan," he taunted the corpse. "Made yourself famous, did you? Well, they'll be singin' 'bout Bucky Perry from here on out."

"Sure, they will," Pinto said, dragging himself away from the door.

"Ain't just anyone can kill himself a whole family," Perry added, aiming the rifle at Brax.

"Not dis day!" Pinto said, throwing himself at the outlaw. The rifle flew one way, and Pinto rolled the other with young Perry flailing away at him. For a moment Pinto screamed as the young outlaw clawed and kicked, tormenting the mustanger's shattered leg. Then Pinto's fingers gripped the holstered Colt and drew it out. The barrel jabbed its way between two of Perry's ribs and exploded.

"You kilt me," the young man said as blood trickled from his lips. He coughed once, then died.

Jared Richardson raced into the house to find Elsie and Ben laboring over Pinto's leg. Truett hovered over Brax and hugged Winnie to his side.

"Horses comin'," Jared announced nervously. Pinto's eyes fogged, and he ground his teeth.

"Rifle," he told Ben.

"No, wait," Ben urged as Pinto swung the barrel out the window and prepared to open fire at the shadowy figures approaching the house at full gallop.

"It's Pa!" Jared shouted.

Pinto blinked smoke and dust from his eyes and stared in relief as Sheriff Diggs leaped off his horse and bounded into the smoke-filled farmhouse.

"All's over now, Sheriff," Pinto managed to mutter as he collapsed.

"Joe Hannigan," Diggs declared. "And Pat's yonder in the woodpile. This 'un?"

"Thought to make himself a name," Pinto said. "And I don't even remember it. Four more down by de cornfield."

"And two at the road," Ryan Richardson added as he draped an arm around his son. The others then set about dragging the bodies from the shambles of a house. Pinto lay on the kitchen table and let Elsie bind his leg.

"You came," Truett whispered as pain shot up Pinto's side.

"Guess I'm not such a lone wolf as I figured. huh?" Pinto asked.

"Long as you're figurin' things, is it time to call up a preacher?" Elsie asked as she examined Pinto's arm.

"Buryin' kind?" Pinto said, studying her eyes as pain ate at him.

"Marryin' kind," she said, grinning.

"Might as well marry you while he buries them Hannigans," Truett suggested.

"Might's well," Pinto agreed. "If it's what you want, Elsie."

"Always was," she answered. "And I judge, with two bullets to get cut from your hide, you won't be in any shape to run away!"

"No need," he told her. "I'm home."